HOUSE OF THE TALKING CAT [Temp. Trolley]

HOUSE OF THE TALKING CAT

stories by

J.C. Sturm

STEELE ROBERTS
AOTEAROA NEW ZEALAND

For Jim, Hilary and John

First published in 1983 by a Spiral collective — Irihapeti Ramsden, Marian Evans and Miriama Evans, with assistance from Anna Keir, Juliet Krautschun, Kathleen Johnson and Pauline Neale; and Joy Cowley whose generous help was given in gratitude for over twenty years of support from women writers. The first edition, with the same cover illustration by John Baxter and design by Basia Smolnicki, was published with financial assistance from the New Zealand Literary Fund and reprinted in 1986 by Spiral in association with Hodder & Stoughton.

Acknowledgments are due to *Numbers; Te Ao Hou; NZ Short Stories,* second series, edited by C.K. Stead (OUP); *Into the world of light,* edited by Witi Ihimaera and D.S. Long (Heinemann); and *Mellan tua varldar,* edited by Bengt Dagrin (Forfattaves Bokmaskin), where some of these stories have already appeared.

We thank Colin Bassett and Bronwyn Bannister for assistance with this new edition.

This edition published in 2003 by Roger Steele

STEELE ROBERTS LTD
BOX 9321 WELLINGTON, AOTEAROA NEW ZEALAND
phone +64 4 499 0044 • fax +64 4 499 0056
books@publish.net.nz • www.publish.net.nz
1-877338-06-0

Contents

"For memory is so often a single explosion,
like a firework in the mind. One is blinded."
JANET FRAME *The Edge of the Alphabet*

"Yes, but the order of the imagination
is not that of memory."
LAWRENCE DURRELL *Balthazar*

I

The Bankrupts

They both arrived punctually at the appointed place but on opposite sides of the street, and seeing each other in one and the same instant in spite of the crowd and early evening traffic, they bridged the gap between with smiles a little too bright and mouthed greetings and hands raised awkwardly — something they had never done before. The girl stepped off the pavement, then back again as the man hurried across to join her.

"Hullo, how are you? I'm glad you could come, it's good to see you again."

"Yes, isn't it? … I mean, I'm glad I could come too." She was still smiling, but nervously, a little flustered. "I hope I haven't kept you waiting. The picture bus is sometimes late."

"No, no, not a minute, you're dead on time. I wouldn't have minded if you had anyway." He offered her a cigarette.

"No thanks, not just now."

"Are you sure?" He lit his own, and drew on it sharply and heavily.

"Well, what have you been doing with yourself since I saw you last, anything exciting?" She pulled a face.

"No, nothing, just the same old routine. Could anything exciting happen in this … this morgue of a place? By the way, did you manage to get seats for that film I was telling you about?"

"No, I didn't as a matter of fact, but I don't think we'll have any difficulty getting in if we want to. But there's plenty of time and the shorts are bound to be a bore. How about walking as far as the gardens and back? It's almost too good a night to spend in a stuffy theatre, don't you think?"

"Yes, I suppose so," she said doubtfully, looking over her shoulder at the town clock pointing to quarter to eight.

Evelyn liked the gardens. She always had. Even in the daytime with gardeners sweeping and planting out, and children sprawling round the fountain basin willing the goldfish to come, and middle-aged women with thermos flasks and knitting twittering among the sparrows, and young things in overalls from the laundry across the way giggling and nudging each other under the trees and throwing their fish and chip papers and pie-crusts and half-eaten sandwiches under the seats for someone else to pick up, and old men with watch chains and walking sticks wheezing and blowing like so many stranded bullfrogs and staring and staring and sometimes hawking as you went past — even in the daytime it was a pleasant shortcut to work, somewhere quiet to wait for a bus, or to have lunch. But in the evening and later it was different. The daytime people went off with the sparrows, and if they came back in the dark, they came back different, with new clothes and new faces and new voices, or no voices at all, and they did what they came to do in the shadows under the trees and never thought of the things they had done there earlier that day. And if they hadn't come to stay but were on their way to the pictures or a meeting or a friend's place or simply to look in the shop windows, it was still a pleasant shortcut, and no one could stop them passing through unless they wanted to be stopped, for this was a public thoroughfare and not the kind of gardens that close at dusk. And if they weren't in a hurry to do something or go somewhere they could wander up and down the paths till they came to the fountain reigning in the centre, and stand there then, and see the neat flower beds flowering into an unexpected exotic brilliance under the moth-haunted lights, and the lawn around the beds wet emerald, and the cypresses taller and slimmer than they were in the sunlight, and beyond them a pattern of tree-shadows, then shadows only and no pattern (and into those they wouldn't stare too long unless something inside them stirred and whispered — *look*), and beyond that the trees themselves — oak walnut loquat and magnolia, beech birch and one jacaranda — huge and solid with darkness from their deep buried root foundations to a living, imperceptibly changing skyline.

"Charming place," laughed Michael shortly, glancing about him, "just like a pretty woman who will charm you and charm you but won't or can't take the matter any further." Evelyn winced slightly. She had been on the verge of telling him about the garden, the refuge it had sometimes been in her early teens, the feeling of ownership she had towards it because her father had been head gardener for years before he retired. But after that laugh it was impossible to say any of it. Not that it mattered. Some people liked city gardens, and others, like Michael, preferred remote beaches, all spray-salted tussock and shingle, and surf-pounded rocks beset with unpredictable currents — places difficult to come to and a relief to leave. That was all very well, and Evelyn found them exciting too, but if you didn't have a wild beach, a tame garden was better than nothing.

"It's better than nothing," she said out loud.

"Yes, I suppose so," he agreed quietly, after a pause, "and at least it's a hide-out from the crowds and nosey-parkers." A group of youngsters in jeans and jumpers whistled and gestured at them from a nearby seat.

"Or is it?" he added ruefully. Evelyn looked annoyed and embarrassed. "Friends of yours?" he teased. She shook her head vigorously.

"No, not that way, come here," and she led him down a path that took them away from the mocking teenagers. It wasn't until they sat down that she realised that she had chosen the most secluded spot in the gardens where they could be seen only by people passing within two feet of them, and perhaps not even then.

"Well, this really is a hide-out," said Michael with surprise. "How did you come to find it?"

Because my father used to eat his lunch here every day, Evelyn answered inside herself, and out loud — "Oh, I know every inch of this place and all the advantages and disadvantages of each seat. I thought this would fool those young wolves if they try to track us down."

"Mmm," mused Michael, not looking at her, "I don't think they will. That's probably their night stand and they'll stay there till dark and give couples the works as they go by. But never mind about them." He half turned towards her. "Now, tell me what's the matter. You look worried about something. In fact, if you don't mind my saying so, you look downright miserable." Evelyn looked down at her hands and floundered for words. Michael was always surprising her like this. He never seemed to take much notice of other people's reactions and moods. He was attentive, yes, and considerate, but not the watch-you-and-weigh-you-up type at all. And then he would suddenly make it plain that he was aware of how she was feeling, and she would find herself telling him all about whatever it was, self-consciously at first, then with confidence and relief. But this time, what could she say? The trouble had been lying in ambush for them at the bus stop (who knew how long — an hour, a day, or since the beginning of their friendship?) and now was hunting them down surely with small arrows of indecision and a net of silence. Would they escape if they could? Why had he evaded the pictures and she agreed to the gardens instead, and this seat, had she really chosen it because of those cheeky kids? Michael touched her on the arm. He was offering her a cigarette.

"Thanks." She avoided his hand as he held out a match. "It's just the same old story, trouble at home."

"Is it?"

She hurried on.

"It depresses me to see them, two people who have spent most of their lives together allowing unimportant trifles to undermine their marriage. Wouldn't you think, with the end in sight for both of them, that they would pool their resources, draw closer together for strength and comfort, and — and love one another as never before? But no, not a bit of it. Every day they grow more irritable and impatient and critical, accusing each other of petty persecutions, and when they remember the past it's only to revive old grudges and resentments. They have nothing left to share but a sour discontent, and no interest for anything that doesn't directly affect them. I want to shake them, shout at them, do something to wake them up before it's too late."

"You mustn't be too hard on them, Evelyn, they're no worse than most people. That sort of thing can happen to anyone, and very often does."

"I know, I know, but that only makes it worse. No one is immune, nothing can stand against it. No matter what we are or do or have, time is bound to creep up and steal it from us in the end. We are all potential bankrupts. I tell you, Michael, it terrifies me, the thought of getting old like that. I hate it more than anything else."

"Well, you've got quite a while to go before you need worry about grey hair and wrinkles, and a lot of other things to do before business goes bust," Michael said lightly, and the amusement in his voice made her feel a little foolish. All she had said was true and the feeling she had put into the words was sincere. But right at the moment none of it seemed terribly important, and Michael knew it, and she couldn't pretend any longer that it was. What really mattered was the two of them sitting together, and Michael's arm resting along the back of the seat behind her shoulders, and the garden with all its perfumes and shadows, colours and lamps, ready at last to receive the night. Evelyn felt something small and soft brush against her throat, and looked down in time to see a moth disappear inside the front of her dress.

"What's wrong?" said Michael, leaning towards her as though to look too, but Evelyn jumped up, loosened the belt at her waist, and shook herself vigorously till the moth half-flew, half-fell from beneath her skirt. Michael threw back his head and hooted with laughter.

"Now," said Evelyn drily, when he had finished, "I wonder why it would want to do a thing like that?"

"For the novelty," suggested Michael, laughing again. "But to return to your old age," he said, suddenly serious once more, "people who are afraid of growing old usually feel they are missing something and will go on missing it till it's too late." He withdrew his arm and went on almost brusquely. "You want to stop that kind of thinking before it becomes a habit — find out what's missing and do something about it." Evelyn sat perfectly still and said nothing. They were silent for a while.

"Are you cold?" asked Michael, turning to her.

"No, are you?"

"No, but my backside's numb with sitting on this hard seat." He glanced at his watch. "It's too late for the pictures and too early for supper." He stood up slowly and looked down at her. "How about coming back to my place for a while?" Evelyn stared straight ahead while her heart and head fought for the right to reply. *Say no, you shouldn't go. Why not, don't you want to? That doesn't matter. What else does? Everything. But what difference will it make? All the difference in the world and you know it. But you're good friends, aren't you? Not any longer. Aren't you jumping to conclusions? No, I'm not, and it's time you stopped pretending. You're the one who does all the pretending, pretending for weeks that it couldn't happen, and now that it has, pretending it's not what you want. I say again that doesn't matter. And I say it does. You'll be sorry. And I'll be sorrier if I say no.* Evelyn heard her own voice speaking scarcely above a whisper.

"I've never been before."

"I know, we've always done something else."

"Couldn't we do something else now?"

"What?"

Evelyn was silent again. She stood up.

"All right," she said, not looking at him, and began walking back the way they had come.

The small room was more comfortable than she had expected. The floor was covered with wall-to-wall floral body carpet. A reading lamp was fixed to the wall above the bed, and another light hung over a glass-topped dresser standing before a large mirror. A towel rail and handbasin with hot and cold water filled the corner opposite the wardrobe, and between them a window opened over the street below. Evelyn peeped out cautiously, feeling strangely safe behind the curtains, like a patient admitted to hospital at last.

"Nice room, Michael."

"Yes, isn't it?" His voice was muffled by the wardrobe where he was rummaging for something.

"What are you looking for?"

"Something to drink … I'm sure I had … yes, here it is." He backed out with half a bottle of gin in his hand. "Have one?" Evelyn hesitated a second.

"Yes, please." She watched him rinse a couple of glasses and mix the drinks. "What would your landlord say if he knew I was here? You know I felt like a thief creeping up the stairs behind you."

He shrugged carelessly.

"Well, you needn't have. He doesn't live on the premises."

"What about the other people in the house?"

"Too busy minding their own business." He handed her a glass and clinked his own against it. "Cheers. Now for goodness sake sit down and make yourself comfortable and relax, you still look worried. Drink that down and I'll get you another." Evelyn sat on the edge of the bed and watched the serious, rather strained young woman in the mirror slowly drain her glass. And suddenly she felt limp with enormous relief. They were here. After the skirmishing in the gardens, the awful silent retreat, the fear of being stopped by a friend in the street, the guilt on the stair, after all that, and in spite of themselves, they were here.

"We've arrived," she said loudly, and sat up very straight and looked round the room as though she were making an announcement. Michael leaned against the wall and watched her curiously.

"Yes," he said slowly, "and it's taken us a damn long time to get here." They looked at each other for a moment and burst out laughing. Evelyn held out her glass to be refilled.

"Wasn't it awful in the gardens, I couldn't think of a thing to say."

"So you burbled away about growing old."

"Did you mind very much?"

"No. I knew you would soon dry up." They laughed again, and Evelyn wriggled back on the bed and patted the space beside her.

"Stop propping up that wall, and for goodness sake sit down and make yourself comfortable and relax." He smiled and sat down.

"You don't look worried any more."

"I'm not… But you should have taken me to the pictures."

"Good God, haven't you forgotten that yet? I had no intention of taking you to the pictures."

"I know. But what am I going to say when they ask me what it was like?"

"Tell them it was a flop, and change the subject." Evelyn held her glass up to the light and squinted through it.

"You know," she began slowly, "we're a funny family, and I don't mean funny ha ha, either." She paused a minute, then frowned and finished her drink impatiently instead of going on. "Don't let's talk about them any more, we might as well be in the gardens still." Michael put her empty glass on the dresser and sat down beside her again. Evelyn looked at herself, dress spread out and slightly crumpled, legs straight out in front of her, feet dangling over the edge of the bed. She watched her shoes drop off one by one. Michael ran his hand thoughtfully down the line of her arm from elbow to fingertips.

"Cold?"

"No."

"Then why are you shivering?"

"Am I? I didn't know." She looked at him stretched out beside her. "You've got new pants on."

"Yes."

"And a new shirt?" She let her hand rest lightly on his shoulder.

"Nearly," he murmured, taking her in his arms and kissing her, gently.

"You know," she said, lying back and looking at the ceiling, "I think I've wanted you for quite a long time." He smiled down at her.

"And I've wanted you for years and years."

"I don't believe that, but it doesn't matter." She sat up on the edge of the bed, swinging her legs and staring at him in the mirror.

"I think I'll have another drink, but before I do, have you got anything?"

"Any what?"

"You know, something. I don't want to end up in a nursing home." He gave her a half amused, half admiring look.

"Don't worry, you won't."

"But are you sure it's good?" she persisted.

"Positive. Now forget about it."

"Well, pour me another gin while I get out of these," and she undid her dress and pulled it over her head. Michael stayed where he was, watching her.

"I suppose I'll have to take everything off, but I wish I didn't."

"Why not? You've got a beautiful body."

"No, I haven't. My breasts are too small and floppy. See …" and she shook her shoulders slightly. Michael pulled her down beside him and kissed her as though he were searching for something.

"You've still got your tie on," she said shakily, loosening the knot, "you'd better take it off in case I choke you. And this. And these." She stood up, filled her glass, emptied it, and shook her head at the carpet dizzy with flowers.

"Evelyn, are you all right? You'd better go easy on that bottle. I don't want you with your head in a basin for the rest of the night."

"No, I'm feeling fine, but I think I'll have to go to the lavatory." She dragged her dress over her head again. "Now tell me exactly where it is. I once read a story where the man had to leave his girlfriend to go for a leak, and he spent the rest of the night trying to find his way back to the room. And he never did." She looked as though she were going to cry.

"Michael, it would be terrible, I couldn't bear it." He shook with laughter.

"All right then, listen carefully. Go down the passage that way, turn to the right, and it's the first on the left." She nodded gravely. "And if you're not back in five minutes, I'll stick my head out the door."

Only the reading lamp was glowing above the bed when she returned, expanding the room, pushing its walls back into shadows and giving it a new height and depth and character. Just like the gardens at night, she thought, and stopped as though someone had called her name. Michael was sitting on the bed holding an empty glass between his knees.

"I'm glad you're back," he said quietly, not looking at her. "I was beginning to think you really had got lost. Or even run away."

"How could I without these?" she laughed, dropping her dress on top of the rest of her clothes. She knelt in front of him and pulled his shoes and socks off. "Did you forget about them?" she said, rubbing her cheek against his knee. Michael put his glass down, ran his fingers through her hair, and cupped her face in his hands. She smiled up at him. "This makes me feel like a Rodin statue, the one called 'The Kiss', do you know it? Terribly romantic, but the real thing, not a bit sentimental. I wouldn't mind being romantic if I could be like that." Michael held his arms out with an agonised look and slid slowly off the bed towards her. They collapsed in a heap, on the floor, laughing and holding each other. Then Michael suddenly tensed, as though in pain or anger, and caught her up, and laid her on the bed, and reached for the light switch without taking his eyes off her face. And his hands and mouth ransacked every room in her body till they found what they wanted, and Evelyn slipped from his arms into a roaring blackness, crying his name aloud for fear of losing him.

The brightly-lit street was startlingly quiet and completely deserted when they let themselves out carefully through the front door. Evelyn looked about her unbelievingly. Same place, same night, nothing changed. She wouldn't have been at all surprised to find her little world transformed — houses jumbled into a crazy new pattern, trees ablaze with magic coloured lights, pavements trembling to the thunder of an unseen ocean triumphantly besieging the outskirts of the town. But everything was just the same as they had left it, except that all the people had vanished.

"I can't make it out, Michael, where's everybody gone? I've never seen the place so empty before." She hugged his arm. "Perhaps they've fled before us." He nodded absent-mindedly.

"It's probably later than you think." She stopped dead.

"Good heavens, I'd forgotten all about the time. What is it?"

"Don't know, I left my watch behind. But we'll be able to see the clock round the next corner." Evelyn hurried ahead.

"But it can't be that," she gasped, turning round and clutching his arm. "We've been away hours." He nodded again as though he were still thinking of something else. "Michael, whatever shall I do? What will I say when I get home? They're bound to be waiting up for me."

"Tell them we went to a grill room for supper after the pictures, and got talking and forgot the time. Say as little as possible and be as casual as you can. And don't tell lies — you're bound to trip up in the end if you do." She walked along soberly for a while.

"But I won't let them spoil everything," she said suddenly, turning to him, "I won't, they have no right to." Michael put his arm around her.

"No," he said gently, "they haven't, and they won't. Just remember and they won't be able to touch you." She clung to him, shivering and hiding her face against his shoulder. He stroked her hair.

"Now we'd better find you a taxi. There should be one under the clock. But before you go, there's something I want to ask you. I …" he hesitated, trying to find the right words. "Evelyn, I hope you're not … are you angry with me?" She lifted her head in amazement.

"Angry with you? Whatever do you mean? Why should I be angry with

17

you?" She put her arms around his neck. "Didn't I make it plain that I …
that I …" Michael caught her close and kissed her as though their time
together was only just beginning, and neither of them heeded the light-
hungry moths giving themselves gladly to the burning lamp above.

A Thousand and One Nights

They spent the afternoon on the small front lawn under the gum tree overlooking the harbour. It was more sheltered on the side lawn but the grass round there was stiff and prickly and you couldn't see the harbour, so the woman spread the rug at the foot of the gum tree and sat with her back against the trunk and her knitting in her lap. And all afternoon she pretended they were simply warming themselves in the gentle autumn sun in front of an old house hidden away in bush with a harbour to look at, and all afternoon she knew they were simply pretending and none of it was real, not even the wanting and willing and pretending, nothing except the waiting. The little girl squatted on her haunches at the edge of a garden shabby with withered summer flowers and talked to herself and mixed mud pies in an old enamel bowl and put in gravel for sultanas and baked them in tin lids and iced them with daisy petals and laid them beside the woman on the rug. Are they cooked yet, Mummy? And the woman felt each one with a finger and said, what pretty daisy cakes, yes, I think they're cooked, but we won't eat them, they're too pretty to eat.

And when it was three o'clock and time to waken the toddler, they hid the daisy cakes first, just in case, and went up the gravel path and wooden front steps and down the long linoleum passage past the mirror in the old coat-stand that wasn't theirs, past the white china door knobs of the bedroom, sitting-room, breakfast room, past the old ship's bell on a fretwork bracket hanging at the end of the passage, and round the corner and through the door that always stuck and had to be pushed. And there was the toddler pulling himself up by the bars of the cot and his cheeks were plump and pink and his eyes blank with sleep. They changed him and put on rompers and jersey and carried him out to the gum tree and he blinked and blinked in the gentle sunlight till his eyes were as round and as blue as the harbour, and the little girl laughed and rolled on the rug against the woman's legs and laughed, he's Hunca Munca, Mummy, he's turned into Hunca Munca.

They made a pretend picnic with orange drinks and biscuits and pieces of apple and the toddler rubbed his in his hair and got it mixed up with bits of grass and stones till it looked like a piece of daisy cake and the little girl watched him and said, aren't toddlers silly, Mummy, and ate hers carefully like a tea party lady. And then she pulled off the little white boots she wore to make her ankles grow straight and strong and galloped around the lawn like the horse she was and stopped at the far end where the bush began and held up her arms like branches. Look, I'm a tree, you can't get me now, I'm a tree. And the toddler dropped his daisy cake and staggered and gurgled and fell and crawled and dribbled across the lawn. But when he got there the tree turned into a bird and flew away. The woman leaned against the gum tree and watched them and pretended it was all real, but the sun slipped behind the tallest trees in the bush and the shadows crept across the corner of the rug and it was four o'clock.

They gathered everything up except the daisy cakes and put them on the side verandah and went round to the clothesline on the back lawn where the sun still shone and the little girl said, we don't have to go in yet, do we Mummy, it's still warm and sunny here, but the woman shook her head, no, it's getting late, it's time to light the fire and put the dinner on, and she gathered an armful of soft fluffy napkins and dropped the pegs for the little girl to pick up and gave the toddler a nappy to carry. And while they were picking up pegs and folding napkins and the toddler got his tangled round his legs and fell over and had to be untangled and picked up too — while they were busy dawdling in the last of the sun, the cold crept out of the bush on the other side of the house and hid in the darkened rooms waiting for them.

The little girl squatted on her haunches outside the woodshed and peered in the corners for wetas, and the woman poked about inside the shed turning the wood over and feeling it to see if it was dry and keeping a lookout for wetas too, and the toddler climbed up and down the concrete steps and looked at them upside down between his legs like Eeyore. And when they had carried the wood into the sitting-room and filled up the woodbox and the coal-scuttle and found the matches, the woman stuffed newspaper in the grate and jumbled dry sticks on top of it and covered them up with the heavier stuff and lumps of coal and held a burning match to the paper at each corner and dropped it in the middle. But the wood wasn't dry enough and smoked, so the woman covered the fireplace with another newspaper and pressed the edges hard against the bricks and the little girl looked stern, now you Mr Fire, you just burn up that nice wood my Mummy's given you, and don't be silly. And the toddler sat very still and watched the newspaper and waited. And when they heard a low roaring behind the paper and something began sucking its middle inwards the woman pulled it away quickly because she never knew what to do with it when it caught alight, but there was only a small flame after all struggling against the smoke and the heavy damp wood.

By five o'clock the children were in the bath and while the little girl was showing the toddler how to make waves for the boats to float over and the ducks to swim over and how to spread your flannel out flat on your knees like this to rub the soap on, the woman set about cooking the meal. She cooked enough for four. And then she carried the children into the sitting-room in big fluffy towels and rubbed them down in front of the fire and put on their warmed pyjamas and dressing gowns and slippers. The little girl struggled to do up her own buttons and pushed and pulled at them and pulled her face down to see them properly and asked the woman is Daddy coming home for dinner, and the woman turned away to look at the clock and shook her head slowly, no, dinner's ready now, so he can't be. Can't we wait for him? He might be very late. Do all Daddies come home after dinner? Some do and some don't, and if they do, they can't help it. If my bunny slippers had teeth they could bite. And she moved her toes to make the ears wiggle and the toddler gurgled and tried to make his wriggle too. Don't forget to pull the blind down, Mummy. And the woman went over to the window and tried not to think of the face that had been there once, a terrible dead white face with everything dragged down — hair, eyes, nose, mouth — pressing to reach them through the glass, till the toddler covered his eyes with his hands and the little girl screamed and screamed and hid herself in her Daddy's coat when he came in soon after. The Daddy laughed and said it must have been the moon come down to see them, but the toddler wouldn't take his hands away till they played peep-bo with him. So the woman pulled the blind down carefully right below the sill and picked up the towels and went out to the kitchen. And when she had served up four dinners and put the biggest one on top of a pot of hot water on the stove and covered it with a plate, she took the other three into the sitting-room and they had their dinner round the fire, the little girl sitting on a cushion with her red table across her knees and her bunnies wiggling at her on the other side, the toddler safe in his low chair with a feeder, and the woman beside him, just in case, with her plate in her lap.

And when they had had enough and drunk their milk, the woman stoked up the fire and dragged up the biggest chair in the room and the little girl brought her favourite book and the three of them squeezed into the big chair and made themselves comfortable for the story of Tom Thumb and his wife Hunca Munca. The little girl liked the story so much she knew what was coming over the page and said it out loud with the woman, and the toddler wanted to pat the pictures and dribble on them and got so excited his cheeks puffed out and his eyes were as round and as dark as Hunca Munca's. And when they had finished the last page they read it again slowly and loudly because they liked it so much and the toddler didn't know it was finished and went on puffing and patting and the little girl gave a great big sigh and stared into the fire. But what was the use of Tom Thumb putting a crooked sixpence into the doll's stocking and Hunca Munca sweeping the doll's house every morning, Mummy, when they'd smashed everything up? Weren't they silly mice to smash up the doll's house just because some of the things weren't real? And the woman said, yes, very silly, but perhaps they didn't know any better, being just mice. She carried the toddler into his cot and tucked them both up as snug as a bug in a rug and the little girl said night-night, Mummy, and say night-night to Daddy when he comes home, and the woman said, yes, I will, night-night and sleep tight. And it was nearly seven o'clock.

She washed the dishes and put the things away and turned off the stove under the pot with the dinner on top and went back to the sitting-room and turned the radio on and settled down with her knitting. But that wasn't any good because she couldn't hear anything except the noise it was making even when it was turned down low. So she found a book and settled down to read but that wasn't any good either because when she'd read a page twice carefully she still didn't know what she'd been reading. So she found a pencil and tried again, underlining bits here and there and writing things in the margin and this time it worked — she could read and underline and write things and *listen* at the same time. And the later it grew the easier she felt because if he hadn't come by eight o'clock it would probably be midnight or the early hours of the morning, that's if he came at all. So the reading got easier and she didn't write so much or listen so hard, but by ten o'clock the fire had burnt right down and the woodbox and coal-scuttle were empty and she couldn't be bothered going out to the woodshed because of the wetas. She thought of having a bath but it seemed a bit risky — a bath wasn't a good place to be caught in — so she made some supper instead and filled her hot water bottle and got ready for bed.

But she didn't want to go to bed in case it happened again. She put her book and knitting away and straightened the chairs and cushions in the sitting-room and straightened the towels in the bathroom and swept the hearth and made sure there were enough aired nappies for tomorrow and picked up the children's toys and put them in the box on the side verandah. And when there weren't any more things to do she tiptoed down the passage and round the corner, and lifted the handle so the door wouldn't stick and jar and crept in, but there wasn't anything to do there either except gaze at the children so pink and plump and easy in their sleep. So she crept out again and stood in the passage and didn't know what to do. If she went to bed it might happen again, and if she stayed up she might be caught. She stared at the old ship's bell and wondered what would happen if she took it down and stood on the front steps and shut her eyes and swung it up and down up and down with both hands as hard as she could — no, that wouldn't do because the children might wake up, and they mustn't find out — then suppose she ran through the bush with it and stood in the middle of the road and rang it and rang it till she couldn't hear anything couldn't listen to anything except the ringing. Would the people in the brown house with the white facings and the sunken garden and the people in the one next to it with the tennis court and the people in the new two-storeyed home with the sundeck and the people who lived at the end of the long wide drive, would they look at one another and say, listen, isn't that someone ringing a bell? Why would anyone want to ring a bell in the middle of the night? And if they left their houses and came out to her, cautiously, in the middle of the road and asked, what are you doing, what is the matter, and she told them, this is an old ship's bell that hangs at the end of the passage. It doesn't belong to me, but I'm ringing it now because I've been waiting a long long time and I'm still waiting and *I can't wait any longer* — the woman put a hand to her mouth — what would they say then, what would they do with her then? She turned away from the bell and got into bed and waited and listened.

And some time later, she didn't know what time and it didn't matter because the waiting was over, she felt the footsteps thudding through her sleep, down the steps from the road into the bush, under the macrocarpa trees, past the giant fuchsia peeling its brown paper bark in the dark, between the bamboos in the dip beside the stream, into the tree-tunnel that led to the house. She slipped out of bed and crept across the passage into the sitting-room and hid behind the door, and the footsteps thundered around the house and into the house and up the passage and stopped suddenly outside the door. *You don't know I'm here, go to bed, I'm not here.* But the door swung open and the footsteps came in and closed it and stood there for a time and when they turned round it was the face at the window, dead white and terrible and all dragged down, pressing to reach her and there wasn't any glass *there wasn't any glass.* And the woman covered her eyes with her hands and screamed and screamed and tried to hide herself in the wall, and woke with the screams choking her and the bedclothes pressing her down and her body shaking and clammy with the thudding of her heart.

And then she heard the footsteps again coming through the tree-tunnel, heavy and uncertain at the same time, and then she couldn't hear them at all. Perhaps he's pissing against the gum tree, perhaps he's gone off the lawn and fallen down the bank — no, not the bank, I can't do it, it's too far down and too far up and the pungas get in the way, please not the bank — let it be the gum tree. And she waited and listened and the footsteps came back on to the path and around the house and into the house and tried to be quiet up the passage. And she lay like someone hiding behind a door and shut her eyes and breathed deeply and slowly, I'm asleep, I'm asleep, and listened to the fumblings on the other side of the bed and the clothes dropping and the hands groping and felt the pull on the bedclothes and the mattress sag and listened till the breathing beside her was slower and deeper than her own. And she lay for a long time in the small space between one waiting and the next and felt everything but the tiredness drain away from her, and listened to the small night noises and the night wind and watched the gum tree through the window, moving its branches like arms against the pale night sky — if you could turn into a bird, you could fly away — and she watched the gum tree, waiting for the miracle, till her eyes ached and closed and it was over.

Where to, Lady?

It was my day off, or strictly speaking, my afternoon off. Not given, you understand, just taken. The best kind, I told myself defiantly, walking firmly down the path, walking out on the house, the family, a long long week of 'life's responsibilities', and turning a cold shoulder to the ones ahead. How many of them between now and then I wondered glumly on the road. Never mind. It's high time I made a gesture and I stood beside the Russian Embassy perched on the brink of the city and gathered myself together for the plunge. I should be Joyce Cary, I thought, looking down at the harbour, then I might be able to translate all this into words. Maybe a huge earthenware bowl with a chipped rim and a puddle of pale blue milk in the bottom, would do. Maybe. Anyway, no matter how you looked at it, it was a perfect day, one right out of the box, all clean and fresh and carefully ironed hanging up ready for somebody to step into. That's me, I said right out loud, and I ran down the steps and picked up a tram.

But it's never as simple as that. I mean, you just can't move out of one world and into another simply by boarding a tram. For one thing it's usually a help if you know where you want to get off. And I didn't. Sitting in a tram not knowing where you are going and waiting for the conductor to come is nearly as exciting, and much more pleasant, than sitting in a tram knowing where you want to go, and knowing too that it doesn't make much odds because you haven't got enough money in your purse anyway. So you just sit quietly waiting for the conductor to notice you while the tram covers miles and miles of line, and you pass the time away wondering what you'll say to him and what he'll say to you, and whether he'll take your word and your address, or whether he'll tip you out at the next stop, both of you red in the face with indignation, and leave you stranded and acutely ashamed about being ashamed.

"Where to, Lady?" asked the man himself, bringing my reflection on trams and conductors to an abrupt end.

"Where to?" I echoed, searching his face hopefully for the answer.

"Yes, lady, that's what I said," and he looked patiently out of the window over my head.

"Oh, the cenotaph," I suggested, "that's if you go that way." Well, I thought, as the tram cast me high and dry on the small island of grass and concrete, of all places in the world, why did I have to choose this? And I walked round the monument examining it carefully for the first time in my life. Maybe the day could do with a memorial, but not this one. I might just as well have settled on the sphinx. I turned my back on the pile of stone and bronze and made for my nearest friends.

The wife wasn't wearing lipstick because a mosquito had bitten her on the lip, and the heat of their upstairs flat had made her a little vague, but there was nothing the matter with her welcome. She just stood in the doorway and smiled.

"What a pretty dress," said the man as I walked into the living-room, and he did some deft juggling with a baby, a book, and a teddybear. "How clever of you to wear a girdle instead of a belt, much more becoming with that, and your sandals — my dear, where did you get those sandals?"

"Yes, isn't it, aren't I?" I smiled, and sat down because that's what he really had said. The room steadied itself around me. Books, books everywhere. And pictures. Every conceivable size, shape, and colour, of book and picture. But it was the pile of cushions that held me fast. There seemed to be dozens of them, every one a different colour, all clustered gaily on a dark navy couch like so many miraculous flowers in winter, while behind them hung a long, graceful, gently moving yellow curtain.

"Oh, beautiful," I murmured, forgetting the cenotaph.

"Well, not quite," said the wife, smiling tenderly at the baby, "but she's beginning to look almost human. The poor wee thing hasn't been sleeping very well lately. She doesn't know how to cope with mosquitoes yet, and this heat makes her so cross."

"Me too," I said ruefully, flapping the front of my dress for coolness.

"Like some tea? We drink it all day."

"I'd love some," and I tried to think back over the years to my last meal.

"Take a look at this," said the man offering me his open book, and there it was, all spread out before me at last, another world. Tiny blue figures that could have been human, dwarfed by immense black symbols and gold animals, and between them, immeasurable space, space everywhere.

"Their cosmology is amazing, absolutely amazing," he told me, "and you wouldn't believe it but it works. I mean it draws all the strands together, shuts all the doors, answers all the questions, tells them everything they need to know in this world or any other, and finally directs the whole. Can you imagine it?"

"No," I replied, shivering slightly. "No, I'm afraid that kind of living is quite beyond me, not my cup of tea at all." The wife appeared carrying a tea tray and began to conjure innumerable cups out of a doll-sized teapot. "Now this," I said, picking up a book of short stories I knew better than any friends, "this is different, this is what I can imagine." And all the pain and passion, discoveries and loss, waiting and disappointments, the unending unanswerable questions, and the unwanted final statement, crept from between the covers and nestled in my hand. "Some book," I said "and what a woman. I wish I knew how she does it," and I watched the baby grasp handfuls of nothing from the air above her head, examine them intently then kick and coo with delight at the wonder of it all.

"Oh that," he said, rearranging baby and bear. "Why can't people in this country write about what they know now, instead of something somebody knew fifty years ago, or something they hope we might understand when we've grown up? Honestly, you'd think life was a sequence from a Kafka novel. Wouldn't you?" and he looked across at me suddenly with suspicion.

"Nice cake," I said to the woman. "Did you make it?"

"Of course she did, she makes all our cake. Wonderful cook. Wonderful woman." And he grinned up at his smiling wife, jigging the baby between them.

"Well, I really think I'd better go," I said slowly.

"Must you?" asked the woman, breaking the tableau. "I thought you meant to stay to tea," and the three of us roared with laughter. "We've got pumpkin pie. Lots of it."

"Good heavens, pumpkin pie. I've not even heard the name for years and years." And the book I was still holding dissolved into an American magazine open at a double page of incredibly coloured foods with a huge pumpkin pie sitting triumphantly in the middle, and my mother was telling me …

"No, no," I said, getting up hastily, "I've imposed my appetite upon you too many times. I really must go home. After all it's getting rather stupid."

"What did you say?"

"I mean it's rather stupid to stay when it's obviously going to rain and I'm wearing only this," I explained, shaking my light dress. There was no doubt about the rain. The room was still warm, but had darkened with the sky, and the three of us seemed slowly drifting apart on a sea of shadows, our faces growing paler and indistinct, and our words too ineffectual to measure the distance. Only the yellow curtain billowing above the cushions remained.

The rain was coming down steadily at the first tram stop, and no tram in sight, so I walked slowly up town, taking shelter under the shop verandahs. The street was scattered with people like me, sauntering along with nowhere in particular to go, window shopping, talking and laughing, filling in their Sunday afternoon, or making the most of it. I could have been any one of them. A group of young bloods came towards me, speaking to each other quickly in a language I didn't understand. Immigrants, I guessed, looking at their solid rubber-soled shoes, their long slicked-back hair, their long dazzling ties, their long straight jackets, their … , that's enough of that, I ended grimly, bringing myself up with a jerk, and I turned my attention to a menu outside a crowded milk bar. Eggs, mince, sausages, pies, spaghetti, no fish, and I moved on. "Oh you'll *never* get away, you'll never *get* away, you'll never get *away, you'll never get away,*" gloated the jukebox after me. Is that so, I thought, watching my tram approach, pause, gather speed again, and disappear slowly, slowly round the far corner.

The library was closed 5.30pm – 6.30pm. The milkbars were overcrowded or had their jukeboxes going full blast. Even the bus timetable read no bus. I was almost in despair when I found myself outside a grill room, not one of those brassy, glassy, we-can-offer-you-anything-you-want-with-fluorescent-lighting restaurants, but a poky, cheap-looking, open-twenty-four-hours-a-day kind of joint, just one degree better than a pie cart, and definitely grubby. Oh no, I panicked, not here, of all places, please not here. And my mind reeled back to a different age, and a different me standing on the same spot with another all lost forever a lifetime ago. When I came to I was staring wide-eyed at a man sitting at one of the tables just inside the door. One cheek was bulging with food, but he had stopped chewing and was regarding me with growing interest and a certain amount of expectation. I knew what he was seeing. An odd young woman, who looked as though she had just been touched by a ghost, standing in the rain without a coat, taking hours to read a menu written on the window in large white letters and plain English. There was only one thing to do. I walked in.

The small room seemed full of men all shovelling food into themselves as fast as they possibly could, but at one of the side tables sat a half-caste Maori woman by herself, and as I hesitated in the doorway she pulled out the chair beside her and nodded to me.

"Takes you a while to make up your mind," she smiled as I sat down. "You looked kind of funny standing out there in the rain."

"I bet I did," I said, feeling my face go red. "I don't often do this, I mean, I'm not used to having meals in town. I usually cook them myself." A waiter slid through the back curtain like a ferret and sidled over to me.

"Yes, lady," he smiled into my lap, "and what do you fancy?"

"Oysters, please."

"Sorry, lady, no oysters."

"Whitebait, then," I said, forgetting the time of the year.

"Sorry, lady, no whitebait swimming around these days."

"Well," I said, leaning back in my chair, "what can you offer me?"

"Eggs, mince, sausages, pies, spaghetti."

"No thanks," I shook my head desperately, as the room began to spin.

"How about a little sole with salad?" he whispered, his smile sliding to ankle level.

"Oh, that will do fine," I sighed with relief, and he brought me the largest, flattest flat-fish I had ever seen lying on a plate.

"Nearly all bones, honey," chuckled the woman, as she caught my expression, "and I ought to know. I cook hundreds of 'em a week. I'm third cook at the City Club Hotel," she finished with dignity.

"Good job?" I prompted through my fish.

"Not bad, at least the work's all right. I like to cook. But the people — these low-class pakehas who think they know everything — ugh! The lady-boss, she's okay. She's hard as nails but she's fair. She says to me, do what you're paid to do, that's all I want, the rest is over to you, so when the kitchenhands start any dirty nigger business I get my slap in first. I'm not going to be pushed out of a good job by any silly so-and-sos. Would you?" She picked up her plate and walked out the back before I could say anything. Dirty nigger, I wondered, as I watched her go. Not by any possible manipulation of the words or their meaning could I make the description fit. She was a large woman, a little stout, but well-corseted and with a good posture. She was wearing a black and white gold-printed ever-glaze frock, with a fitting bodice and a very full skirt, the kind of dress I had admired hundreds of times in shop windows. Her court shoes, like the handbag she had left lying on the table in front of me, were good plain black. Well-dressed by anybody's standards, if you cared to apply them. Not that clothes or posture or even dignity are any protection, I thought wearily, if somebody wants to call you a nigger. She looked a little flustered and embarrassed when she came back from the kitchen.

"Going any place tonight?" she finally asked me.

"Not really. I had thought of going to the library, but it's not important," I replied, wondering what was coming next. There was a long pause.

"Well, look, things are in an awful mess out there. There's a rush on as you can see, and they're short-handed. They want me to help out with the dishes and they thought you might keep me company." I turned my sole over carefully.

"I don't know," I said slowly. "I really should be getting home, but I suppose, for a little while …"

"Good," she said, not waiting for me to finish, "I thought you would." A ferret was hiding behind the curtain when we went through.

"Pleased to see you, lady," he grinned, offering my lips a cigarette.

"Come and meet the boys and make yourself at home." You could hardly move for bodies and food and dirty dishes, and the steamy heat and smell of burning fat was almost overpowering. One side of the room was taken up by a huge sink and bench, while along the other side were gas rings, a steel grill, and a wooden table where the cook, sweat running down his face, was working like a madman. We tied dirty aprons round our waists, took a deep breath, and started. For nearly an hour we went flat out, shovelling dishes in and out of the sink, stacking them in drying racks, washing and shredding lettuce and slicing tomatoes. Home, I thought ruefully, was never like this. When things had slackened off a bit the woman and I went out to the nearly empty dining-room to cool off.

"On the house, ladies," sang the ferret, banging down glasses and two bottles of raspberry fizz, "just call for more when you run dry."

"Gawd, my feet," sighed the woman, drinking her fizz steadily. "Some night out you're having, honey," and she smiled uncertainly at me.

"I'll say," I said, feeling sticky and smelly and dirty. "I've just about had it. Anyway, I'd better get back to the family."

"Family?" she said, putting down her glass. "You got kids?"

"Only two."

"What you done with them?" she asked me sternly.

"My husband's at home. He's minding."

"What?" and she burst out laughing.

"Where's the joke?" I asked, on the defensive.

"Oh nothing," she said, wiping her eyes, "but they won't all come at that game, you know, honey. You're a lucky one. What happened? Walk out on him?"

"Sort of. But only for the afternoon." She burst out laughing again.

"Well, you've got the right idea, anyway. Break 'em in young. Show him you can still stick up for yourself."

"I suppose so," I said, collecting the empty bottles and glasses, "but I hadn't thought of it that way."

Back in the kitchen the woman and the cook started ragging each other.

"You must be crazy crawling into a hole like this with that dress on," and he eyed her bosom critically.

"Want me to take it off?" she threw back at him. "Anyway, you can't be too bright yourself, taking a job here. What you doing it for?"

"Money," he said, patting his pocket, "they don't give you anything else these days. You wouldn't believe it, but I used to run a show like this myself once. Made a little pile of eight thousand. Then I settled down quietly in a pub and blew it all in three years. So here I am, starting all over again. Got two jobs to hurry things along, this all night and another all day. Keeps me healthy. But money never worries me. Now women," and he smacked his lips together like a goldfish, "I like 'em." And God help 'em, I thought, taking in the short wiry hair, sharp blue eyes, rat-trap of a mouth, the whole stocky strength of the man.

"What, back again, kiddo?" he asked, catching my stare. "I thought you'd turned it in."

"Oh, it's early yet," I said, running the tap.

"Sure. But you don't want to strain yourself. What do they call you, kiddo?"

"Sally, when I'm good."

"And when you're bad?"

"They don't call me anything. They don't even know me."

"Too bad," and he looked at me thoughtfully. "Say, that's a pretty dress you've got on. I like that kind of tie thing round the middle." His hands were busy feeling for lumps of fish in a big enamel bowl of batter.

"Want to know something, Sally? You ought to come to town more often. Drop in anytime." The ferret slipped between us, curled himself around me, and dropped a clean plate in the sink.

"Sure," I said, turning away. "I might do just that." Kafka, I thought savagely. Kafka nothing.

"I've changed my mind. I'm going now," I told the ferret.

"Hold your horses, there's no hurry."

"There's plenty of hurry. I can hear the kids howling."

"Okay, okay." He shrugged his shoulders and reached for the phone.

"Calling you," he crooned, "there's a little lady here wants to go home. What are the chances?" There was a pause while his grin slowly widened.

"Could I?" he smirked all down the front of himself "or could I?" He ushered me through the door, winking broadly at the others.

"See you next Sunday?" he asked when we got outside. "Say yes, and I'll get off early. How about it?"

"Can't make it," I said, wishing the taxi would come.

"Aw come on, break it down. You can't treat a guy like that."

"Oh can't I?" I said, facing him squarely as the taxi drew up. "Look, I'll let you know what my husband says."

And I climbed into the back seat.

A pity, I thought, as he slammed the door without a smile. After all, ten bob, raspberry fizz, cigarette, sole with salad. Maybe he lives alone in one room without a hotpoint. Maybe he's got six kids and a sick wife. Maybe I look like a girlfriend who let him down. Maybe. I tapped the driver on the shoulder.

"Where to, lady?" he asked through his *Sports Post*.

"Where to?" I echoed. "Home." And I sat back, shutting my eyes against the city lights.

The Dance

The first turning without a street light wasn't what they were looking for. The tarseal led purposefully to a wall of summer-dry shoulder-high stiff pale grasses, and there stopped.

"Open Sesame!" challenged Derek, striding forward. Priscilla watched him coldly — what a fool her husband was — but the others laughed, and Vivienne, blonde blue-eyed slightly tipsy Vivienne, laughed loudest of all. The footpath wasn't much better. It dropped its respectability among the grasses, gave the Boy Scouts hall a wide berth, and lost itself completely to an unmarked weed-erupting tennis court. Vivienne waltzed into the middle and gazed around.

"This can't be it. There isn't an orchestra." Derek bounded forward with a whoop, twisted himself through the movements of a service, darted forward to smash back the return, vaulted lightly over the net that wasn't there, and shook hands heartily with Vivienne, who was waiting for him on the other side. Everyone laughed again, except Priscilla, who was already halfway back to the road.

"Come on you two. That's unless you want to spend the night here, playing tennis," called Jane over her shoulder. Not that she'd mind. She was holding hands with Terry and as they moved round the corner of the hall he drew her closer and gave her hand a squeeze. But he was thinking of Vivienne. He was damned lucky to have such an attractive wife, and God knows, after two children in five years, not counting the one that died, she deserved a good time. Only he wished she wasn't drinking so fast. She was liable to take too much at times like this and get herself upset. He'd have to watch her. They caught up with Mary and John who were still trying to decide which of them should go home early to give their first baby a bottle. Mary was wearing a new dress and reckoned she should be the one to stay. Further ahead, Jane's husband, Bill, was making no headway with Priscilla who was straining her ears for sounds from the tennis court.

Back on the main road they couldn't understand how they'd missed the hall the first time. Noise washed out of the open door and splashed from the high sash windows, yellow with light, over a few bicycles sprawling against the walls, on the gravel below. A tide of voices rose and fell and heaved and swelled to break with a shout on the thump, thump, thump, thump, and uncertain wail of an orchestra.

"What is this, anyway?" grinned Bill, "a dance or a military drill hall?" Priscilla shrugged. She had dragged through one of these nights before.

"You'll soon find out." Jane, still holding onto Terry's hand, was peering through the back windows of one of the cars lining the street.

"What's up?" asked Terry. "Belong to a friend of yours?"

"Not that I know of. I just wanted to see if they had parked or were parking. Once I found a couple going it hammer and tongs, doors wide open, right in the main street. Anyone could see." Terry looked at her. Jane laughed and jerked his hand.

"And don't try to look shocked. Now if I had a car, or better still, if you had a car …"

"You deserve to be …"

"I know. I hope I am." The music rushed to a climax, hung there, then strolled down a few chords on the piano as though it couldn't care less. A woman's voice shrilled out a question that wasn't answered.

"What's it all in aid of?" asked John.

"What's what in aid of?"

"All this, the rumpus, the dance, or whatever they call it." A wave of his arm took in the hall, couples drifting out the door for a breather, Terry and Jane standing under a light beside the cars. Priscilla shrugged her shoulders again. It was a habit of hers.

"Don't ask me. A new sandpit for the kiddies, a paddling pool six by six, money for the old folks not at home — something like that. Chalk it up for charitable purposes if it's bothering you." She glanced along the street, then away again quickly when she saw Vivienne and Derek bouncing up, arm in arm, looking very pleased with themselves.

"Finished the set," shouted Derek, "and I beat hell out of her. She's out of practice, Terry. You want to watch out, old man, one day you'll wake up and find she's found another coach." Vivienne hung on his arm and laughed, her eyes large and bright and her cheeks flushed. God, thought Jane, doesn't she ever stop laughing?

"Well, what's the hold-up? What are we waiting for? If you chaps came to stand outside and keep your hair tidy, I didn't," and Derek leapt up the stairs half-carrying half-dragging Vivienne with him. Terry sighed and felt through his pockets for the tickets.

There was a crush in the ladies' cloakroom, and no pegs left to hang coats. It smelt strongly of perfume and face-powder and taffeta and B.O. and woollen overcoats and the lavatory that wouldn't flush. Priscilla was first in and first out. Vivienne hadn't bothered to come. Mary readjusted the belt of her new blue dress and stood on her toes, craning over and round the other women to catch a glimpse of the neckline in the mirror. Jane elbowed her way right up to the glass and started powdering her face.

"Well, if it isn't Jane Taylor, only you're Jane someone else now, aren't you? Fancy meeting you here. I don't suppose you remember me." Jane turned round quickly. She had a good memory for voices and knew this one perfectly well, but it wasn't saying the right kind of things. It should have been chanting silence please girls keep to the left no talking on the stairs hurry up three professional keep in line silence please girls. On and on and on.

"Yes, of course I remember you. You were Phyllis Thompson at high school. You've not changed much."

"But you have, Jane, you're a lot thinner. I suppose your young family keeps you busy. Someone told me at the last old girls' reunion that you were married with a baby — by the way, do you ever go back to the old school? — no — well, you should you know. It gives me such a thrill to sit in the old hall again and walk up the stairs and along the corridors and look out of the library windows past the wattle tree over the playing fields. It all seems like yesterday doesn't it?" She gave a little smile and a little sigh. "And how old is your baby now? Goodness, why it can't be, I mean, you haven't been married that long have you? Doreen must have made a mistake. Do you remember Doreen? She was in the same year as us. And …"

Jane cut in smoothly and coolly. "No, Doreen didn't make a mistake. And don't you remember, we weren't in the same year. I was only a squinty little third-former when you were a prefect in the sixth and took corridor duty. We were worlds apart. There must be at least three or four years between us." Jane turned back to the mirror in time to see Phyllis give her a long hard look. There was a sudden quiet. Most of the other women had gone out and there was a lull between dances in the hall. The prefect and the cheeky little third-former stared at each other in the glass.

"Fancy making a mistake like that, I must have been thinking of the basketball team. We were in the 'A' together, weren't we?" said Phyllis finally recovering herself. "Well, I'd better go back and see what my hubby's up to. He doesn't really enjoy this sort of thing very much. And I must say it's not quite what I expected. I think there's a lot to be said for a little formality at a dance, don't you? Bye-bye, I'll probably see you later." Bye-bye, thought Jane, powdering her nose again without knowing it, I'll probably see you later — in hell. The bitch. Of course she knew when I was married. Trust her to check up on dates. She was annoyed to find her hands fumbling as she put the compact back in her handbag. So what. She'd go out and find Terry and have another drink.

She found him near the bar at the other end of the hall, standing with a bottle of beer open in his hand and talking to a man she didn't know. Without a word, she took the bottle from him and tilted it up for a long drink.

"Well, well, doesn't the lady like drinking out of a glass?" said the man watching her. Jane lowered the bottle and stared at him.

"What the hell's it got to do with you how I drink, or whether I drink or …" Terry grinned and took her by the arm.

"She's not one to waste time on glasses. Come on, let's dance for a change." Jane tried to relax into step but something had gone wrong.

"What's up?" murmured Terry, not looking at her.

"Oh, nothing. I just met an old school-tie in the cloakroom and …"

"I know. And she raved about those wonderful old days and wonderful old Miss Sourapples who tried to teach you maths. And the wonderful smell of chalk dust and watered-down ink and the cloakrooms in wet weather, and the wonderful old whats-it tree that used to bloom all through exam time. And then she gave you the lowdown on all the wonderful old girls, and wound up with a verse from the wonderful old school song. Right?" Jane was laughing in spite of herself, with a queer shaky feeling inside. She moved closer and found the step and the beat at last.

"Terry," she said.

"What?"

"Nothing." He smiled. Derek whizzed Vivienne past with a noise like a fire siren. Terry watched them go.

"The kid's having a good time," he said.

"Looks like it." Jane could see Bill with a fixed vacant smile carefully steering Priscilla round the outside. Both of them looked bored stiff. Jane didn't know who was worse off — Bill talking to Priscilla, who wouldn't talk, or Priscilla dancing with Bill, who couldn't dance. Mary and John were sitting it out. John wasn't a dancer, but Mary's foot was keeping time to the music as she watched the crowd swing by.

"I'd better dance with Mary soon. If she sits there much longer she'll turn into a frying pan and John will be the sausage."

"Let him burn." Jane liked dancing with Terry much more than she liked Mary. Back at the bar after the dance the men were mixing punch in a crock for salting down beans. Derek was passing out the drinks over heads. He had taken his coat off and his shirt was sticking to him in damp patches.

"How much is this costing you?" asked Priscilla.

"Bob a time."

"It's sheer robbery."

"Well, you won't be needing much of it."

"Indeed. Since when have you bothered to notice how drink affects me? So far you've spent the entire evening showing off."

"Oh, shut up." Derek drained his glass and elbowed his way to the door. Vivienne was whispering excitedly in Jane's ear.

"And then what do you think he said?"

"Can't imagine."

"He said I look like the cover of a French novel." Jane looked at the wide blue eyes and full mouth, the fair hair falling loosely to the shoulders of the low-cut black dress.

"Then what?"

"Oh, he said a lot of other things, but I thought the bit about the French novel was the best."

"All depends on what you think of French novels. You'd better watch your step, Derek's as tight as a drum." Vivienne giggled.

"I've had quite a few myself."

"That's what I mean." Jane turned away irritably. What a fool the girl was. What was it Terry could see in her that no one else could?

"Take your partners for the supper waltz," bawled the M.C. Things were beginning to warm up. Most of the crowd round the bar were pretty high, the men shouting and pushing for more drinks, and the women smiling and talking brilliantly to no one in particular. The members of the orchestra had taken their coats off and were grimly defending their music stands against the press. A middle-aged woman in a pink dress and an orange party hat stood in a puddle of punch and broken glass and wept and sagged helplessly against her partner who was stroking her down with a fixed glassy smile. I didn't mean to do it I didn't I don't know why. There there never mind of course you didn't just hold on tight to me. The pianist swept the debris off the piano, muttering to himself, and pounded into the Merry Widow waltz. Jane sipped her punch, wondering where Terry was.

"Excuse me. May I have the pleasure of this dance?" Jane turned round in time to steady a man who was trying to bow to her. She glanced about quickly but Terry still wasn't in sight.

"Of course," she smiled brightly, stepping into his arms. "Haven't we met before?"

"Never," he shook his head slowly and sadly, "but I've often seen you on the bus."

"What bus?"

"The bus I drive." Jane laughed.

"Do you drive as well as you dance?"

"Much much better. You don't mind, do you?"

"Mind what?"

"Mind dancing with me. You're such a beautiful dancer. I've never danced with anyone like you before. What are we supposed to be doing?" Something wailed past them like a railcar.

"Look," said Jane, "there's a man with a horn." He held her out at arm's length, startled.

"What did you say?" Jane laughed up at him.

"I said, look, there's a man with a horn."

"Now, if you were a lady —"

"Who said I'm a lady?" He pulled her closer.

"Do you know what?"

"What?"

"I want to kiss you." Out of the corner of her eye Jane could see Phyllis Thompson with her coat on, watching. Jane reached up and kissed the man lightly on the cheek.

"Come with me. I want you to meet a friend of mine," and she led him by the hand to where John was sitting by himself.

"Hello," said John, taking the situation in at a glance, "what have you been up to?" Jane sat down with her back half-turned on the man, and lit a cigarette.

"Where's everybody? Where's Mary?" John pulled a face.

"She's gone home to feed the baby. She always gets mad at me at dos like this because I can't dance. I suppose I should have gone, but, hell, I'm sick of babies and bottles and nappies, and going home early and getting up in the middle of the night." Jane nodded sympathetically.

"And where's Bill?"

"He said he felt like a walk. The others are down by the door. Supper's coming out. Want to join them?" Jane glanced at the bus driver as they went. He was slumped against the wall smiling tenderly and murmuring to himself, I want to kiss you, I want to kiss you, I want to kiss you.

When they reached the others, Derek was just finishing one of his funny stories.

"And ever since then I never see anything pink hanging down but I want to pull it." He reached up and grabbed at a paper streamer fluttering above his head. Vivienne hung on his arm and giggled adoringly. Terry was watching Priscilla's face stiffen with anger.

"For heaven's sake, Derek, pull yourself together, you're drunk. I think it's time we went home. I've got a splitting headache …"

"*So* you want to take *me* home, and give *me* aspirins, and put *me* to bed, to cure *your* bloody headache." He glared at her. "I've had enough of your bloody nagging. Why can't you leave me alone? Whenever you open your bloody mouth it's Derek, you've been drinking too much, Derek, why don't you do this, Derek, why haven't you done something else. I hate the sound of your bloody voice." Priscilla faced him, white with humiliation.

"Derek, don't make a scene here. Please. Will you find me something to eat?"

"Certainly, madam. Anything you say, madam," and he backed away bowing with mock politeness. There was an awkward silence and Vivienne looked scared. Jane tried to fill in the gap by telling them about the bus driver but it didn't seem funny any longer. Derek came stalking back and bowed low before Priscilla over a plate of saveloys, pink and steaming and half out of their skins.

"Could madam toy with one of these? Oh, a thousand apologies, I forgot madam can't bear the sight of them." He shoved the plate into Bill's hands and made for the exit, pulling Vivienne after him. Priscilla walked away to the cloakroom without a word. Jane touched Terry's arm.

"Terry, don't you think you'd better go and see?" He shook his head.

"No, it's all right, he's too tight. If he has any more, and he's probably emptying that flask of his right now, he'll pass out. I could do with a drink myself after that lot. How about you?"

The punch had turned cloudy and bitter. Jane sipped hers with distaste. What a hell of a night. The orchestra was plugging away at Latin American while a conga line coiled and stamped and broke and rejoined round the floor. A woman screamed as her dress ripped at the waist.

"Better than a football scrum," grinned John. "I hope the kiddies and the old folks appreciate our effort. Hello, here's Vivienne back. What's up?" She was making straight for them across the floor, pushing her way desperately through the dancers. Terry hurried to meet her.

"Vivienne. What's wrong, darling? What happened?" He put his arm around her.

"Derek tried to kiss me at the top of the steps outside, and lost his balance — and fell down backwards and cut his head at the bottom. There was blood everywhere. And then he was sick. It was awful. Bill found us and fetched Priscilla and she went for me like a wild thing and said I'd spoiled the evening for everyone and made Derek drunk on purpose and was trying to break up their marriage. Terry, I didn't really, I didn't mean any harm."

"Of course not, dear. Where are they now?"

"They've gone. Bill called a cab." She was shivering.

"Terry, let's go home." They met Bill at the door.

"Thanks, Bill," said Terry quietly.

"That's okay. You might have to do the same for me some time. God, that woman's got a tongue." Terry nodded, and helped Vivienne into her coat.

"Let's walk a bit. I could do with some fresh air."

They turned down the main road in silence, Terry and Vivienne walking ahead.

"You know, John," said Bill, "I can't make it out. Just before supper I came out for a breather, and I got it into my head that I wanted to find that tennis court again. But do you think I could? I must have wandered round for half an hour. I found a turning I thought was the right one, but it only took me to the back yard of a fruit shop full of old banana crates and rubbish tins and I nearly cut my throat on a clothesline in the dark. I can't understand it. I'm coming back here one day and I'll go over the area with a fine-toothed comb." He was silent for a while. "That tennis court," he went on slowly, "it bothers me. It was like — well, it was like something we'd all had a long time ago but forgotten so that we couldn't even recognise it when we found it again. A sort of lost garden. Do you know what I mean? Did you feel anything of that?"

"Can't say I did," replied John, "but then I've not got much feeling for places. It was certainly quiet and peaceful though, especially if you compare it with the dance." He laughed, "if you can call it a dance." Jane was walking ahead of them, humming to herself and trying to balance on the edge of the gutter. Trust Bill to lose a tennis court and then get worried in case it was the Garden of Eden. In front of her Vivienne began sobbing softly. I shouldn't have come, Terry, I should have stayed at home. It didn't work, it never does, nothing works any more since the baby. Terry had his arm tight around her and was stroking her hair and murmuring softly. Jane stopped and watched them go. She looked back to where John was waiting while Bill lit a cigarette. He was frowning slightly and so intent on shielding his handful of light and warmth against the wind that he didn't notice a dark narrow turning on the other side of the road, that led to a footpath and a tennis court hidden away in tall grasses pale under the moon.

The Earrings

Helen examined her face anxiously in the mirror, leaning so close to the glass that it misted over and she had to rub it clear with a handkerchief before she could see herself again. She passed the tips of her fingers lightly along the curving line from ear to chin, feeling carefully for any roughness or blemishes, and frowning when she found them. Of course, on this day of all days, she had to have a skin the colour and texture of pumice. She must start taking molasses and iron tablets again and have more early nights — yes, that most of all, but for the time being a cover-up with cream and powder would have to do. She frowned again, then stopped immediately and tried to smooth out the lines creasing her forehead and the furrow that puckered the space between her eyebrows. Nice eyes, she thought gratefully, and eyebrows that looked finely plucked but never had been. Nice mouth too, but her hand shook a little as she began stroking on the lipstick, so that the outline of the upper lip wasn't quite true and the lower lip had a lopsided look about it. She glanced at her watch. No time to start all over again. She'd probably be late already, and he hated to be kept waiting. She looked at her reflection critically in the full-length mirror as she clipped on the wide elastic belt that was rather flashy but helped to give her straight up and down, almost flat, figure a bit of shape. It doesn't matter how good the brassiere is, she thought, looking at herself side-on, if you haven't got enough to put into them, you haven't, and that's all there is to it. Gloves, handbag, shoes to match, clean hankie, seams straight. What else? She hesitated before the mirror. Would she or wouldn't she? The last thing she wanted was to look overdressed or got-up specially for the occasion, but quickly she took a jeweller's small cardboard box out of the top drawer and screwed on the pair of long drop earrings that lay lightly on the pad of cottonwool. Without another glance at the mirror, she tiptoed from the room and down the passage to the kitchen where her husband had just finished washing-up and was putting away the few lunch things.

"Bill, you're a dear. I hope you didn't mind doing them all by yourself, but I'm terribly late as it is. I'll have to fly." In the back bedroom she could hear the baby thumping about in his cot. "And if Hugh hasn't gone to sleep in about quarter of an hour you might as well get him up and let him play outside or something. And you won't forget his orange drink, will you?" Her husband turned round and grinned at her.

"Go on, off you go, don't stand there giving orders." He looked her up and down, his glance resting for a moment on the glittering earrings.

"Have a good time," he said slowly, with a faint smile, "but mind you're home for tea."

"Of course I will, silly," she laughed, going down the back steps. "Where do you think I'm off to, the South Pole? Bye-bye." And she waved her gloves at him as she ran down the path without looking back. This was the worst part, the going, much worse than the coming back. Poor, dear, kind Bill. Even now it wasn't too late. She could still go back, make some excuse about a headache, take off the earrings and change out of her good clothes, and spend the afternoon in the garden. Goodness knows there was plenty to do. But here she was at the gate, and opening it, and passing through, and shutting it carefully behind her because of little Hugh. The long familiar road looked strange and exciting in the clear spring sunshine, and she found herself noticing details — a newly painted fence, a border of blue hyacinths that hadn't been blooming a week ago, bright curtains with a contemporary design hanging in the long bay windows of an old house — that normally wouldn't have stood out so sharply or seemed so significant. It was almost as though she were walking the footpath for the last time and wanted to hang an accurate picture of the scene in her memory that would never fade — an absurd idea. If I hurry and take the shortcut, she thought, I might pick up a tram to get me there on time, even now.

As the tram swung round the last corner and slowed down at her stop, Helen carefully avoided looking out the window to see if he were waiting. She sat fiddling with her gloves and bag until nearly all the people had got out, but when she finally did go to the door, a frail white-haired old lady in a black hat and a long black coat was still trying to lower herself and her walking-stick down the high step. The driver clanged the bell impatiently. Oh God, thought Helen, one day I'll be like this, shrunken and bent and helpless, frightened of crowds and tram drivers and grateful when some young thing lets me lean on her arm. Nothing on the other side of the street will be nearly as important as simply getting my bones safely through the traffic. The woman gave Helen a timid smile and whispered, thank you, my dear, before she ventured out in the middle of the road. Helen drew a deep breath and straightened her shoulders as she watched her go. A sudden gust of wind curled her hair across her face and whipped her clothes back against the outline of her body. A taxi pulled up at the crossing with a jerk and the driver waved her on with a grin. Yes, some day I'll be like that, but now — and at last she looked across to where she knew he had been standing and watching her all the time.

"You're late," he snapped, scowling down at her. "I've been here nearly half an hour. What happened?"

"I was a bit late with the lunch and then the baby didn't want to go to bed. I'm very sorry," she stammered. This was worse than she had expected.

"Did you tell Bill you were going to meet me?"

"Yes, of course."

"Won't he think it a bit odd?"

"No. Why should he? I often arrange to meet friends in town and have coffee with them," she lied. "Why should he think it odd if I do the same with you?" He shrugged his shoulders impatiently and looked away.

"I think you know what I mean." There was a long silence. They were walking up the main street and Helen suddenly realised that this was the first time they had been together like this, just the two of them, walking along sedately through the town and the heart of an afternoon, as though it were something they were used to doing and could do again any time they chose. She stole a quick glance at him. He was holding himself straighter than usual and the expression on his face was grim as though he had come to an important decision and was bent on putting it into action. She felt a wild flutter of panic. What if he — what if they — but she couldn't bring herself to put the feeling into words. Her hand went up nervously to make sure both precious earrings were still there.

"I've never seen you wearing jewellery before," he said, giving her a sharp critical look.

"As a matter of fact, I don't often wear these," she began, "but today I thought I'd …" She stopped in confusion as she realised what she was about to say. Her legs had gone so stiff she could have been walking on stilts, and her arms had become monstrous leaden appendages, weighing her shoulders down till the back of her neck ached.

44

"Well, where are we going?" he asked, coming to a stop. "What shopping do you have to do?" *What shopping do you have to do?* echoed in her brain. As though she had come to town on this one day to do shopping. She wanted to burst out laughing in his face.

"I haven't anything particular to do," she said, looking round vaguely, "but let's have some coffee, I'm dying for a cup."

The close intimate atmosphere of the small coffee shop, dimly lit by sidelights with smart useless raffia shades, seemed almost indecent after the open bustling street. A proprietor, with a cosmopolitan taste that included Europe and the Far East and the South Seas, had hung his walls with dizzy abstract drapes and oriental masks and life-size Gauguin prints. Helen leaned back in her seat as far away as possible from the narrow strip of red table that separated them. A waitress came forward, smiling warmly, as though the three of them were old friends sharing some secret.

"What will you have?" she asked, cuddling a tray against her hip.

"Coffee for me, please."

"And for me too, please."

"Anything to eat?"

"No thanks," Helen shook her head. The mere thought of food made her throat contract.

"I'll have two coffee cakes." The girl scribbled something on a small pink pad and left them. Alone again. He moved restlessly in his seat, drumming lightly on the table with his fingertips and looking past her through the window that opened on to the street. Helen found herself gazing at a highly polished wooden mask. Under the high rounded forehead, heavy lids drooped over slanted almond-shaped eyes, and the full lips, sharply outlined, were curved slightly in a mocking smile. The whole effect was one of confident nakedness, as though the carver had stripped away all the conventional grimaces and laid the personality bare. For the first time that afternoon, Helen forgot herself.

"Look at that," she said, nodding towards the wall, "what an amazing piece of work. You'd hardly believe that anything so composed and sophisticated could be so primitive and … and savage at the same time," she ended lamely. He glanced at it without interest.

"Doesn't appeal to me much. You see hundreds of them round. Probably done by some suburban housewife trying to escape from the boredom of her spare time." Helen looked down at her hands. The waitress came back and set down two cups of coffee and two plates, each with a small cake stranded in the middle of it. He gave the waitress a black look and started stirring his coffee violently. Helen stared miserably at the offending cake, but said nothing. What was the use? Even if she offered it to him, held it out and said this is yours, you asked for it, please take it, he'd refuse bluntly, or say he'd changed his mind and didn't want it any longer, she could eat it herself. And then it would lie on the table between them while they tried to pretend it wasn't there, and when they'd gone, the waitress would clear it away to the garbage tin or slide it on to a clean plate when no one was looking, ready for the next customer. Helen picked the thing up, and feeling his eyes upon her, bit into it guiltily, too hastily, so that the thin pastry shell cracked and crumbled and a sticky brown caramel filling squirted out and dripped down her chin and the front of her dress. As she wiped her face with the clean hankie and scooped the mess up with a spoon, she could feel the blood rushing to her head, and one of the earrings pinched unbearably. He leaned back in his chair watching her coolly.

"What have you done with the baby?"

"Bill's got the day off and offered to mind for me. He's very good with Hugh."

"I wish I'd known that, I would have come up for lunch and had a yarn with him. I could have got the car for the day but I didn't bother just to come into town. It wasn't worth the trouble of finding parking space." Helen pulled the ashtray towards her, cupping it in her hands, and hung over it like a butt waiting to be stubbed out. There was another strained silence. The couple next to them were leaning on the table, talking softly and eagerly, and smiling into each other's eyes. Their hands nearly touched as they tapped their cigarettes against the same ashtray.

"How much do you reckon it would cost to print a novel in this country?" Helen clung to the ashtray as the words dropped about her like hail. *Why can't you say it outright, shout it at me, deny everything, do anything, only drop this agonising pretence of friendship — we were never friends.* She heard her own voice answering, unbelievably steady.

"It's hard to say. It would depend on so many things — the length of the book, the quality of the paper, the kind of cover you wanted. And, of course, the publisher." But he wasn't even pretending to listen to her reply. He finished his coffee, lit a cigarette, and glanced at his watch. The interview was over. Helen began pulling on her gloves with elaborate care.

"I really must be going. I've got quite a bit of shopping to do before I catch the bus."

"Have you? I thought you said earlier you had nothing to do."

"Did I really?" She looked surprised. "I can't think why. Bill asked me to do one or two things for him, and I must get some oranges for Hugh — they've been very scarce lately — and I want to collect a book from the library." She looked at her watch. "Good heavens, I'll have to fly. Which way are you going?"

"That way," and he jerked his head in the direction. "Which way are you?"

"That way," she jerked her head in the opposite direction and smiled at him. "Well, let's go."

Outside the shop they both came to a stop and stood in the doorway, side by side, staring blankly at the street. They were so close their sleeves were brushing. Just like two strangers, thought Helen, caught together in a crowd, waiting for something to happen — a door to open and let them in, or a ship to slip silently from her moorings. She felt him half turn to her.

"I'm very glad you came," he said quietly and something in his voice, softer than it had been all afternoon, made Helen glance up quickly. He was looking down at her in the old dark way she knew so well. Caught unawares, she could not check the flood of hope before it had swept her heart to her lips and eyes, plain for him to see. Perhaps, even now — but he had turned his head away, and was speaking rapidly, almost irritably.

"And give Bill my regards, will you, and tell him I'll ..."

But Helen didn't hear the rest of the message. She was walking swiftly blindly up the street and round the first corner, where she jerked the earrings off, hardly noticing the small pain, and thrust them deep into her handbag, as though she were thrusting them from her for ever.

House of the Talking Cat

Thomas slipped up the front steps without a sound, paused at the top to glance suspiciously over his shoulder, and hunched himself on the doormat ready for the day to take him in. Hills, trees and houses crept from under the lifting mist and rediscovered themselves. Here and there a lighted window preceded the sun. An early unit clattered to a stop in the valley below and solitary figures, heavily disguised against the cold, stepped like robots through the sliding doors. Thomas twitched his ears as water from the guttering dripped and dripped relentlessly on the concrete path, and suddenly his eyes were all pupil as somewhere in the bush a bird stammered briefly and was dumb. The house still slept behind drawn curtains in a litter of yesterday. Easy chairs huddled foolishly before the lifeless, ash-strewn fireplace. Half a mug of cold coffee, a few paper lollies in a crumpled cellophane bag, quarter of an apple gone brown, a kitchen knife, a packet of cigarettes, letters of protest and enthusiasm already forgotten, cluttered the mantelpiece like souvenirs. The newspaper spread pessimism and wild alarm from the middle of the floor. Those comics, library books, coloured pencils, scribbling blocks, Hornby rails, would never again hold exactly the same positions on the faded green sofa under the window, and that jumble of books, foolscap, carbon paper, dirty ashtrays, unopened bills and magazines, was only cunning camouflage for the large office desk in the corner. The latest paper dart had crashlanded on top of the radiogram, the best of the camellias had fallen. *Shshsh* warned the cold tap from the bathroom at the end of the passage, another day lies in ambush.

The boy in the back room stirred, blinked awake, and looked quickly across at his sister's bed. She was still asleep. He slid from between the warm sheets and crept into the passage, pausing outside the bathroom door with a convulsive shiver — oh, how he wanted to go to the toilet, but it might wake her, and then she was bound to beat him to the front door. And this morning, this morning, he was determined to get there first. Thomas heard him coming, stretched his back legs one after the other, and poised himself on the doorstep, tail up and head down, ready to slip through the crack as soon as it was wide enough, and past whoever opened the door. But the boy was too quick for him and scooped him up, hugging him tightly against his chest.

"Tommy," he muttered fiercely, burying his face in the cold silky fur, "dear Tommy, you're *my* pusscat, remember. You were given to me on my birthday, and you don't belong to *her*." Thomas struggled to free himself, but the boy didn't relax his grip until they were both snuggled under the blankets.

"Stay with me, Tommy," he whispered, holding him with one hand and stroking him heavily with the other, "and we'll play a trick on Jennifer. When she wakes up, I'll hide you under the bedclothes and pretend I'm still asleep, and then she'll go to the front door for nothing." The girl turned over and peered sleepily across the room.

"Is that you, Philip, who are you talking to?" No answer. "Philip, are you awake?" There was a sudden upheaval in the boy's bed as Thomas renewed his struggle at the sound of the girl's voice. "I know you're awake," she said sharply, "so there's no use pretending. And what have you got in bed with you?"

"Nothing," replied the boy sullenly. There was another hump under the blankets, and the girl watched it with a frown.

"I know," she cried triumphantly, raising herself up on one elbow, "it's Thomas." And Thomas quietly bit the hand that was squeezing his stomach into his throat.

"Ouch," exclaimed the boy, snatching his hand away, and Thomas was out on the rug between the two beds, looking like an angry owl.

"Oh, walla warley boy," cooed the girl, throwing back her bedspread, "come and see me, come and be nice and warm." The boy put his thumb in his mouth and watched with a blank face as Thomas leapt on to the girl's bed and burrowed against her.

"There's a dear pusscat," she crooned, fondling his ears, "and were you waiting and waiting outside the front door in the horrid cold and I didn't even know?" The boy jerked his thumb out.

"Jennifer, Cresswell said he's going to bash you after school today." The girl sniffed scornfully.

"Pooh, who's scared of fat old Cresswell? He couldn't hurt a flea, could he, Thomas?"

"Well, I'm just warning you," said the boy grumpily, flinging back his covers, "so you'd better watch out." He stumped into the toilet and slammed the seat up. When he came back the girl was still fondling and crooning, and Thomas was curled up in the curve of her body, purring loudly.

"Wenniper," mimicked the boy in a high sing-song, "be a nice girlie and wead me a storwy."

"Not if you ask me like that," answered the girl crossly. He took a running jump at his bed and Thomas started up nervously.

"There, there," soothed the girl. "Did a silly boy frighten a pusscat? Philip, you know you're not allowed to jump on the bed like that." The boy took no notice of her.

"I'll give you the last penny in my piggy bank if you'll read me a story," he said abruptly, pulling the bedclothes up.

"All right," agreed the girl in surprise, "which one?"

"Any one, it doesn't matter which." The girl leaned out of the bed and groped underneath it for a comic. Thomas crouched lower with flattened ears and stopped purring.

"Thomas, did I squash you?" she cried. "Poor pusscat, I'm very very sorry, I didn't mean to," and she stroked him down with long gentle strokes. The boy jerked his thumb out again.

"But you've got to start reading right away, and keep going till Daddy comes in."

"All right," she bridled, "give me a chance." She opened the tattered paper at random. "*We're lost and the fog's thickening! No one will hear us if we shout for help. What can we do?*" She was halfway through the second comic when the man put his head round the door and told them to get dressed quickly, he'd slept in and it was late.

Thomas was stalking a piece of string in a jungle of chair legs and the man was standing at the bench gulping down a cup of tea when the woman came out to the kitchen in her dressing gown.

"How I hate this rush in the morning," she complained in a tired voice. "I wish to goodness you'd fix the alarm. It's not fair on the kids either." He banged his cup down.

"You don't think I sleep in on purpose, do you? We'll just have to go to bed earlier, that's all." He pulled his coat on and picked up his attaché case.

"You haven't done your hair," she said accusingly.

"I'll do it in the train."

"And what about your lunch?" He turned back from the door impatiently and held out his hand.

"And don't forget it's Jennifer's dancing class this afternoon." But he was gone. Thomas abandoned the hunt and came fawning eagerly about her feet.

"It's no use, Thomas," she said sternly, pushing him away, "everyone wants what you want. You'll just have to wait." He retreated under the table and followed her every move with sharp dark eyes as she measured and mixed cereal, boiled water, cut bread for toast. The girl came out, washed and dressed, her fair hair caught up in a smooth ponytail.

"Mummy, have you seen Thomas? Oh, there you are bwarley. What are you doing under the table? Has he had his breakfast?"

"No, he hasn't. I can't do more than three things at once," answered the woman irritably, "and I wish you wouldn't crawl around the floor like that. Turn on the radio and listen for the correct time." The boy appeared in the doorway, shivering in his underclothes.

"Has Thomas had his breakfast yet?" The woman took a deep breath.

"Philip, how many times have I told you to put your slippers on when you get out of bed, and why aren't you dressed? Go and get your clothes on at once." The boy stood his ground.

"But has he had his breakfast yet?"

"No, he hasn't, and if you don't hurry up you won't be having any either." She lunged at the smoking toaster.

"Mummy," said the girl, coming back from the sitting-room, "I think the man said it's five minutes past eight." The woman nodded.

"I thought so. Here, watch this toast for me while I make the tea — the jug's boiling — and then set the table." She was scooping tinned cat food on to a saucer when the boy came back with his jersey half on.

"Can I give it to him, Mummy? I'm dressed now."

"All right," and she pushed the saucer along the bench and turned round to serve the porridge. The girl darted forward, and while the boy struggled desperately to thrust his arms through the inside-out sleeves, she swept the saucer on to the newspaper beside the back door where Thomas was dancing a frenzied jig on his hind legs. The boy glared up at her, breathing hard and short, clenched fists quivering at his sides.

"I hate you," he exploded, the blood rushing to his face, "and hate you, and hate you." The woman wheeled round with the porridge pot in her hand.

"Now what's wrong? You've hardly got time to have breakfast, let alone quarrel, and Philip, if you get into a rage like that before a meal, you'll make yourself sick." The boy burst into tears.

"It's not fair," he cried, screwing his knuckles into his eyes. "You said I could feed Tommy, and she did it while I was putting on my jersey. She does everything for him, and he doesn't even belong to her, he's mine — mine."

"I do not ..." began the girl, watching her mother out of the corner of her eye.

"Yes, you do, and you tell lies too, and I'm not going to give you my penny now," he shouted between sobs.

"That's enough," said the woman sharply, "and Jennifer, when I say Philip can do something, I mean Philip, not you. If it happens again there'll be trouble." The girl turned away sulkily, fiddling with the buttons on her cardigan. "Now come and have your porridge, and Philip, you can give Thomas some when it's cool." The meal was a gloomy one. The woman kept an eye on the clock and tried to hurry the boy along, but he drooped over the plate and played with the food, while the girl ate quickly and methodically and beat him to the bathroom. The mother kissed them goodbye on the front porch and watched them go down the steps.

"He's very fond of you, Thomas," she said, looking down at him and shaking her head, "too fond. And you don't know it, or perhaps you don't care." He began washing himself vigorously. "And that Jennifer could win over a stone image if she set her mind to it." She went back inside with a sigh.

Thomas was waiting for her at the clothesline when she went out with the washing, and immediately pounced on the peg bag and sprawled himself in it so that she had to feel under his belly whenever she wanted a peg. And while she was on her knees cleaning out the fireplace he pushed his way into her lap and rubbed his head against her arm, so that the ashes fell off the shovel on to the hearth rug instead of the newspaper. And when she went into the front bedroom to make the double bed he was curled up in the middle of it with his paws over his eyes as though he had been there all night and meant to stay there all day. But he couldn't compete with the vacuum cleaner. From the safety of the front porch he watched it through the open door with fearful fascination as it whined and snarled after the woman like some half-tamed beast on a leash.

"And that's that," said the woman at last, "everything's done and we're all nice and tidy in case someone comes." She hesitated in the passage, and Thomas wrapped his tail around his front paws and watched her intently as she stood, listening, with a slight frown, to the silence of the empty house. *Shshsh* hushed the cold tap in the bathroom behind her. Two units groaned away from each other in the valley below. Somewhere in the bush a bird was singing as though he would never have the chance again. She glanced almost furtively into each room as she came slowly to the front door, and looked down at Thomas with a bewildered expression.

"That was queer," she murmured, "and not very pleasant. Just for a moment, Thomas, I felt a stranger in my own house, as though it doesn't belong to me, or I don't belong to it — or something. I don't know." Thomas lifted his chin and blinked up at her sleepily, and suddenly her face relaxed in a smile and she was herself again. "Perhaps it belongs to you, you dopey looking thing. You should have been having your beauty sleep instead of spending the morning trying to put me off my work." She scratched him under the ear. "How about some milk-milk?" He followed her into the kitchen and waited hopefully while she made a cup of coffee and put the biscuit tin on the table.

"Go on," she urged, through a mouthful of shortbread, "there's your milk over there. Have some." But he crouched beside her and stared hungrily at the biscuit in her hand.

"No," she said firmly, turning her head away, "it's the very last piece, and I want it." Thomas stood on his hind legs, placed his front paws on her knee, and meowed. The woman looked down at him reluctantly.

"Oh, all right, here," and she broke off a piece and dropped it on the floor, "but it's no use asking for anything more, that's all I've got to give you. No, you can't come up either," she said, pushing him aside and clearing the things away. "I've got to go to town, and you have to go out."

Thomas was lying in ambush for them when they all came home late that afternoon.

"Oh walla warley boy," cried the girl as he sprang out at their feet and charged up the path to the back door with the boy racing after him.

"It's no use, Thomas," said the woman, dumping her coat and gloves on a chair and putting on an apron, "everybody's hungry, you'll just have to wait till I've got the dinner on. And if you stay there you'll get trodden on."

"Mummy, was my dancing any good today?" asked the girl anxiously as she twirled and postured about the kitchen.

"Mind," warned the woman, dodging round her with a handful of potatoes, "mmm — yes, it was, very good, and you did a lovely arabesque."

53

"Do you really think so? Oh I'm so happy, I want to hug you and hug you," and she danced up behind her mother and seized her round the waist. The woman braced herself against the sink and went on peeling potatoes.

"Have you hung up your coat and put your dancing things away?"

"Not yet."

"Well, I think you'd better. Dinner will be ready soon." The girl let her arms drop and turned away slowly.

"Aren't you nice," she murmured, picking Thomas up and cradling him tenderly, "I think you're the nicest pusscat ever, and I love you very much." She blushed hotly and hid her face in his fur. The woman glanced round with a frown.

"Jennifer, did you hear what I said? And don't rub your face against Thomas like that."

In the sitting-room the boy hovered about the man impatiently as he built up the fire. "Make me a paper dart, Daddy — make me a paper dart, do," he sang, beating time on his father's bent back.

"What's wrong with the one I made last night?"

"Don't you remember, it crashlanded on top of the radiogram."

"Well, I can't do it while I'm fixing the fire, can I? I'll see after dinner if there's time."

"If there's time," repeated the boy disgustedly, jumping up and down on the humpty. "You always say that — if there's time. What *is* time anyway?"

"Don't be silly, you know very well what I mean. And don't jump on the furniture like that. Go and wash your hands and get ready for dinner." The boy scuffed up the runner down the passage and skidded into the bathroom, slamming the door behind him. A few minutes later he bounded out again, his face streaked red and black with watercolour paints.

"Walla walla cat's meat," he whooped, hunting Thomas relentlessly under the table, between the chairs, across the passage, under the beds, into the sitting-room, behind the green sofa.

"Philip!" shrieked the girl.

"Come here!" ordered the man.

"Dinner's ready," called the woman from the kitchen, "time to wash hands."

Thomas stretched himself full-length in front of the fire and blinked at the pale flames darting about the lumps of wood and coal. The children were safe in bed, and the woman in the chair beside him was still and quiet at last, with a book in her lap. The man at the desk dropped the newspaper on the floor and yawned as he rubbed his knees thoughtfully.

"Like a cup of coffee?" The woman shook her head without looking up.

"No thanks, not just now." He left the room and came back with an apple and the kitchen knife.

"You know," he began, dropping the peelings in the fire, "I think we should go out a bit more. How about a film or some kind of show this weekend?"

"Is there anything worth seeing?" asked the woman without enthusiasm, "and where are you going to find a babysitter?" He shrugged his shoulders.

"It was just an idea. Well, how about having some people round for the evening?" The woman moved in her chair impatiently.

"All right. But you can do the asking and make the arrangements for a change." He threw the rest of the apple in the fire, and pulled a bag of lollies out of his pocket.

"Have one?"

"No thanks." He helped himself and pushed the bag along the mantelpiece.

"What's the book, any good?" The woman held it up for a moment, cover towards him, so he could read the title himself.

"Yes, so good I'd like to finish it," she said pointedly, and went on reading. He tilted back in the chair at the desk again and stared gloomily at the litter of books and papers for some time, then gradually his face brightened.

"You know what," he said, forcing a noisy exaggerated yawn, "I think I'm due for an early night," and he glanced sideways at the woman. She remained completely absorbed in her book. He brought the front legs of his chair down with a thump, and Thomas started nervously and looked round.

"Poor pusscat," he soothed in a low voice, "did I wake you up with a fright? Never mind, come and see your father," and he held out a hand and wiggled his fingers. Thomas closed his eyes slowly and turned his head away, on the rug again. The man bent forward and stroked the black striped side rhythmically.

"Be nice," he coaxed, "be nice to your father," and Thomas lay very still while the hand crept round to his belly.

"Oh, what a tum," murmured the man," what a beautiful tawny tum. Does a pusscat like having his beautiful tum stroked?" Thomas growled in his throat and twitched his tail.

"Watch out," warned the woman, looking round, "his tail's going," but the hand kept on, pushing its fingers back and forth, back and forth, through the thick soft fur. Suddenly, Thomas closed his body on it like a jackknife and the man jumped back, laughing and nursing a torn wrist.

"Serves you right," said the woman severely, dropping her book face down on the arm of her chair, "I hope it hurt." Thomas stalked to the door and the woman got up and let him out.

"Now you've driven him out, I hope you're satisfied. Really, you're as bad as Philip, worse in fact, because Philip annoys him with his clumsiness but you …"

"… just annoy him," finished the man, winding a sheet of foolscap into the typewriter.

"I thought you said you were going to bed early," said the woman, watching him.

"Did I? Well, I'm not. I've got enough work here to keep me going all night," and he began typing furiously. The woman picked up her book without another word and went out.

It was well past midnight when the man pushed himself away from the desk and stretched his cramped limbs. The fire had burnt itself out and the room was growing cold. He trod quietly through the sleeping house, gathered an armful of milk bottles from the cupboard under the sink, and let himself out the back door. In the children's bedroom, the boy moved restlessly in his sleep, whimpered, and put his thumb in his mouth. But the girl smiled like a dancer and stretched out an arabesque arm towards the wall. The woman in the double bed clung desperately to her hot water bottle and waited, caught and helpless, in the web of her spinning dream. Someone *was* coming — someone who knew about the shortbread, and nothing less would satisfy them. Outside, the night held its breath, and stiffened silently before the approaching frost. The man paused in the bush and strained his eyes and ears against the leafy darkness.

"Thomas pusscat," he called softly, "it's me, come and see your father. Thomas — Thomas pusscat." There was the faintest rustle in the undergrowth beside him and something soft brushed against his leg. "Thomas," he whispered, groping blindly in the pool of shadows about his feet, "Thomas?" A paw patted his hand lightly once, and was gone.

II

For All The Saints

I hadn't been working long at the hospital before I noticed Alice. She was the kind of person who stands out right away in any crowd, even in an institution where everyone has to wear a nondescript uniform. At first I thought it was her Maori blood — she was at least half-caste — but there were several other Maoris on the staff and a few Rarotongan girls too, so that colour didn't really make much difference unless someone started a fight, and then the important thing was not the kind of person you were but what side you belonged to. But to get back to Alice. If it wasn't colour, I decided, it certainly wasn't glamour either that made her so notable, far from it, though some might have thought her handsome in a dignified statuesque kind of way. She was a tall heavily built woman round about the thirty mark, though it was hard to guess her age, with smooth black hair drawn tightly back into a bun and a smooth pale olive skin that never showed the slightest trace of make-up. Over the usual blue smock we all had to wear, she wore a long shapeless gown, always spotlessly white and just showing her lisle stockings and black button-up shoes. From what I could make out, her work was like her uniform, scrupulously clean and neat and done quietly and methodically without any fuss or bother, in spite of the first cook who would have hustled an elephant. She was the kind of woman boss who is happiest cracking a stockwhip. But even after I had noted these details about Alice and the deliberate way she moved about the kitchen, seldom smiling and never joining in the backchat with the porters, I still wasn't satisfied. I felt there was something else I couldn't recognise or understand because I had never met it before, some indefinable quality that made her quite different from the rest of us.

I was a servery maid in the nurses' dining-room, and my chores often took me across the corridor to the main kitchen where Alice worked. I made overtures whenever I got the chance, offering to help lift things I knew she could manage quite easily by herself, smiling and nodding and generally getting in her way. Nice day, I'd say, or going to be hot again, but never a word back did I get. Sometimes she'd respond with a grunt or smile or scowl, but most times she would just walk away, or worse still, wait silently for me to move on. This went on for several days, but Alice wouldn't be hurried. She had her own way of making introductions.

One morning I went as usual to collect several big enamel milk jugs from the freezer outside the kitchen door — this was my first job every day — and I was just reaching for a jug when *clump* the heavy door slammed shut behind me. I put the jug down very carefully. *Keep still,* someone shouted inside me, as every muscle in my body threatened to batter me against the four inches of door, *don't move, keep still.* I waited till the shouting had stopped, and then I very gingerly approached the barrier and tapped on it timidly like a guilty child outside the headmaster's office. "Are you there?" squeaked a voice I didn't recognise, as though it were using a telephone for the first time. "It's me here, can you hear me?" I waited several lifetimes for the answer that didn't come, then turned away slowly like the lion on the films. Jugs, I thought dully, looking at a wall of them, nice useful harmless things jugs. But at that the whole shelf began to slant and sway drunkenly. I'm at a party, dozens of people around me, talking and laughing and singing and shouting and dancing and stomping to hot boogie woogie. I strained my ears to catch the sound. Drip went a drop of icy water on the concrete in front of me. Now we're all sitting on the floor round a blazing orange fire, eating steaming savs and drinking hot hot coffee and playing a quiet sort of guessing game. I concentrated on a large wooden box against the far wall. How many pounds of boxes to a butter, no, no, how many pounds of — the door swung open slowly behind me, and I crawled back to life and warmth and sanity. Alice was propped up against the kitchen door, tears rolling down her face, and shaking so much with laughter I thought her head would fall off.

"Good joke?" she gasped, while I tried to force my knees to keep me upright. "Funny, eh?" And she gave my shoulder a thump that sent me sprawling into the kitchen like a newborn lamb. From now on, I told myself afterwards, rubbing salt into my wounds, you're going to mind your own darn business. But the next morning when I came on duty, the milk jugs were waiting in the servery. Alice had been to the freezer before me.

After this, Alice and I got on like a house on fire, and it wasn't long before the rest of the staff saw what was happening and started giving me advice. It might have been because they didn't like Alice, or because I was a new chum and as green as they come and they thought I needed protecting, but whatever the reason, several of them took me aside and told me Alice was a woman with bad blood, a treacherous character with the worst temper on God's earth, and the kind of friend who would turn nasty over nothing at all. Soon after, I found out what they really meant and why Alice was the terror of the kitchen.

It had been a particularly trying day, with the thermometer climbing to ninety degrees by mid-morning and staying there, and everybody got so irritable they didn't dare look each other in the eye. I was the last to finish in the servery and thought I'd pop into the kitchen and say goodbye to Alice before I went home. The huge cavern of a place was nearly empty and uncannily quiet. The cooking coppers round the walls had boiled all their strength away, the big steamers that stood higher than a man had hissed their life into the air around them, and the last tide of heat was ebbing slowly from the islands of ovens in the middle of the floor. Alice was alone with her back towards me, mopping the red tiles with long swinging movements, never going over the same place twice, and never missing an inch. As I watched her from the doorway, the little man who worked in the pot-room slipped through a side door and cat-stepped it daintily with exaggeration over the part Alice had just washed. She leaned on the mop and looked at his dirty footmarks with an expressionless face. A minute later he was back again, singing in a weak nasal voice through the top of his head.

"Ah'm a leedool on the lornlee, a leedl on the lornlee sahd." He brushed against Alice and blundered into her bucket so that the soapy water slopped over the sides. "So sorree," he backed away, but he was too late. Alice had him firmly by the coat-collar, lifted him off his clever feet, and shook him up and down as I would shake a duster. As she threw him half the length of the kitchen through the door into the yard, I crept down the corridor, remembering the freezer and feeling that thump on the shoulder again.

But the next day I found out something much more important about Alice than the quality of her temper. She came and asked me if I would write a letter for her. I was a bit surprised and wanted to know why she didn't do it herself. She couldn't. She had never learned to read or write. At first I was incredulous, then as the full significance of the fact sank in, I was horrified. Words like progress civilisation higher standards and free secular compulsory, sprang to their feet in protest.

"Why, Alice, why?"

"My mother was not well when I was a little baby so she gave me to my Auntie who took me way way out in the country and the two of us lived there on Auntie's farm. My Auntie was a very good woman, very kind to me, but she could not read or write and school was too far away so I never learned. I just stayed at home with Auntie and fixed the farm. But one day when I grew big Auntie said to me, we've got no more money Alice, you must go away and work and get some money and bring it back to fix the farm. So I did. And now I am writing to Auntie to say I am getting the money fast and will come back very soon." I tried to guess Alice's age once more, decided on thirty again, and reckoned that 'Auntie' might have been about twenty when Alice was 'given' to her. That made her at least fifty now — getting a bit old for fixing farms.

"You read and write, Jacko?" That was the name she liked to call me.

"Oh yes, I read and write."

"You pretty clever, eh Jacko?" she asked wistfully. "You better show me how."

And so, every afternoon for the next two or three weeks, I tried. The two of us were working the same broken shift from 6.30am to 6.30pm with an hour for lunch and three hours off in the afternoon. We started with writing, but I had to give up, I just couldn't take it. It was far worse than working in the pot-room. Alice would grip the pencil as though it were a prison bar and strain and sweat and grunt and poke out her tongue, and I'd sit beside Alice and strain and sweat and grunt and poke out my tongue. I rummaged around the bookshops down town and eventually found an easy learn-to-read little book, strictly unorthodox, and not crammed with highly coloured pictures of English villages and stiles and shepherds in smocks and meadows with ponds and oak trees and sheep with the wrong kinds of faces and bluebells at the edge of the wood. Our book was illustrated in red, white and black, and the few words on each page were put in little boxes, and you jiggled them round so that each box had a slightly different meaning though the words were nearly the same. I would say — first box: look! here is a dog; the dog's name is Rover. And Alice would repeat it after me slowly, pointing at the right box and looking intently at the words in the picture, and then she would roar with laughter and slap the book and very often me too. It was fun for both of us at the beginning and Alice went ahead like nobody's business, but towards the middle of the book the boxes got bigger and the pictures fewer and the game became hard work. One morning I noticed Alice was looking pale and very glum. Her work in the kitchen was as good as usual but she dragged her feet listlessly and kept her eyes down even when I spoke to her. In the end I asked her what was the matter. At first I thought she wasn't going to answer, and then she burst out ...

"That damn dog, Rover! All night I try to remember what he did when he jumped over the gate, but it was no good, I couldn't think. All night I try to remember and I got no sleep and now I'm tired, Jacko, tired tired." And to my dismay the immobility of her face broke for the first time, wrinkled up like a child's and a tear slipped down her cheek.

"Look, Alice," I said, feeling smaller and more helpless than I'd ever felt before, "you don't want to worry about a silly old dog or a book or reading or anything," and I steered her into the corridor where the sharp kitchen clowns couldn't see her crying. "Look, it's a lovely day. Let's have a holiday this afternoon. Let's pretend it's someone's birthday and have a good time. Oh damn, we can't, it's Sunday. What can we do, Alice?" I waited while she struggled with her voice.

"You do something for me, Jacko? You take me to church tonight, eh?"

She was waiting for me after work. I took one look at her, closed my eyes, and opened them again carefully. She was looking happier and more excited than I had ever seen her, the despair and tiredness of the morning had quite gone, but so had the neat uniform. She was wearing a long pale pink garment that looked suspiciously like a nightgown, and round her neck she had tied a skinny mangy length of fur that even a manx cat wouldn't have looked at twice. But it was the hat that took my breath away. I had only seen such a hat in old photos or magazines about Edwardian England. It was a cream leghorn with a wide flopping brim, dark red roses round the crown, and a huge swaying moulting plume that almost hid her face. I didn't have a hat with me, but I reckoned Alice's would do for the two of us.

"I think I'll go home and see Auntie for a little while. I've got some money for her and when I've fixed the farm I'll come back again." She showed me her suitcase. "I'll catch the 10.30 railcar tonight."

We were a little late for church and as we crept in all eyes swung in our direction and stopped. That's right, I thought, take a good look, you'll never see another like it again. The summer evening sun streamed through the clear glass window and showed up mercilessly, like strong electric light on an ageing face, all the drabness of the grey unadorned walls, the scratches on the varnished pews, the worn patches in the faded red carpets, the dust on the pulpit hangings, and the underlying greenness of the minister's old black suit.

"For all the saints, who from their labours rest," squeaked the small huddle of people like someone locked up in a freezer. I shifted my weight from one foot to the other and leaned against the pew in front of me. Ahmmmahh, droned Alice happily above everyone else except the big-bosomed purple-gowned over-pearled organist, who pulled all her stops out and clung to the top notes like a determined lover. Alice was holding her hymn book upside down.

After the service I took Alice home for supper. She seemed a little lost and rather subdued in our sitting-room, and sat stiffly on the edge of a chair with her knees together and her hands gripping each other in her lap. I made several unsuccessful attempts to put her at ease, and then I noticed she kept glancing sideways at the piano that stood in the corner.

"Would you like to play the piano, Alice?" I suggested. She jumped up immediately with a delighted grin and walked over to the music stool.

"Dadada eedeeda," she sang on one note, and thumped up and down the keyboard. Fifteen minutes later she turned to me. "Pretty good, eh? I know plenty more. You like some more?" And she settled herself down for the rest of the evening before I could reply. My mother got up hastily and went out to the kitchen to make the supper. When the time came to go, Alice looked very solemn and I feared a repetition of the morning crisis. But I was wrong.

"I got something I want to show you, Jacko," she said. "I've never shown anyone before." And she handed me a folded piece of old newspaper. "That's a picture of my uncle. He went away before my Auntie got me. My Auntie says he's the best man she ever knew and one day he'll come back and look after me and Auntie and get money to pay for the house and fix the farm. He's got a good kind face, eh Jacko?" I peered at the blurred photo. A group of men were standing behind a central figure sitting in the foreground, and underneath, the caption read — *"This is the last photo to be taken of the late Lord Tweedsmuir, Governor-General of Canada, well known throughout the English-reading world as the novelist, John Buchan."* My mother looked over my shoulder.

"But surely you've made …" I stopped her with a sharp dig in the ribs.

"Yes, Alice," I said, "he has got a good kind face, and I'm sure he'll come back."

It was bright moonlight at the station. Small groups of people stood around waiting to see others off in a railcar that looked much too small and toylike for the long journey round the foot of the hills that lay to the north-west of the town. Alice gripped my arm till my eyes watered, and then she mistook that for something else and gripped harder still.

"Goodbye, goodbye," she waved out of the window, the plume shedding feathers over everything near her. "See you soon, Jacko, goodbye."

But I never saw Alice again. I stayed on at the hospital for the rest of the summer and then went south to another job, and Alice hadn't returned before I left. Auntie must be sick, I thought, or maybe it's taking her longer to fix the farm than she expected. Several months later I received a letter from my mother. "I've got some news for you," she wrote. "Alice came back not long ago, but her place in the kitchen was taken, so they found her a job in the laundry. She got on all right at first, but soon there was more of the old trouble, and when she nearly strangled one of the other women, things came to a head and they had her put away quietly. There was quite a bit about it in the paper, but of course she wouldn't know that. Poor Alice. Do you remember how she played the piano that night and showed us a photo of her 'uncle'? And oh, my dear, till your dying day, will you ever forget that hat?"

The Walkie-talkie

"*It wasn't hard to imagine what conditions were like inside the heat-tortured Solar Ships. The air would be like the blast from an oven, the water boiling, and the inside surface of the inner hull burning to touch. The best cooling and insulating systems Science could devise, and the special reflector surfaces of the laminated hulls would be no more than a domestic firescreen before the searing sea of pure energy called the Sun. Life would be barely possible. But men did manage to live within the ships, the toughest men in the Galaxy, trained to observe while they struggled to survive, trained to probe within that furnace the secrets of the Phoenix Reaction. And one day discovery would be theirs. They would know at last the mystery of the universe, and then Man could reach for the Stars.*"

"Like a cup of tea, dear? I've just made one. Come and have it out on the front steps." I slapped the *Science Fiction Monthly* face downwards on the arm of my chair. Same old stuff between new glossy covers, dressed up to look like something different, as though life, or death, can be disguised by spacesuits and new dimensions and lethal rays that don't leave a carcass. I got up and went out into the bright sunlight.

The sun was nowhere near its zenith, but already the concrete steps were hot to the touch, and the red climbing roses on the green trellis were hanging limp. The sky had that transparent watery blue look about it, as though it were a bowl of lightly coloured liquid that one could peer through and feel convinced that space held nothing but the sun and our own small planet. I sat down on a step and Les eased himself down carefully on the one below me, passing a hand over his face as he did so.

"Going to be another stinking hot day," he said grimly, screwing his eyes up at the front lawn. Les took a pride in his lawns and tended them carefully, but with the long dry spell and the water restrictions he was finding it a hard job to keep them looking as green and smooth as he liked. He had already been round the small property with his bucket and secateurs, snipping off dead flowers, picking up dropped leaves, and pulling the few weeds that dared to appear in his immaculate garden. After morning tea he would gather vegetables for the midday meal and leave them in neat little piles on the back doorstep — new potatoes, runner beans, carrots and perhaps a young marrow. He works too hard, I thought, he shouldn't do so much in this heat. But what could one do to stop him? Both he and Amy his wife had reached the age where the smallest details of their daily living were vitally important, and to ease off for a little might lead to easing off for good. They did everything with the grim determination of people who know that they won't be able to do it for much longer. A hot wind stirred somewhere at the bottom of the garden and gathered strength as it crept across the lawn, till it burst in full force through the open doors and windows of the house. The whole place shook as the bathroom door slammed, the tinsel and gay glass ornaments on the Christmas tree tinkled frantically, the stiff pink gladioli stirred uneasily in their vase, and photos of the living and the dead flapped helplessly against the wall. Amy tried to keep her grey hair in place and leaned back wearily in the chair, her large body loosely filling the skimpy print dress.

"This damned nor'wester, I hate it," growled Les, watching his wife. "It's worse than the heat, and that's saying something. Amy, did you remember to take your pills this morning?"

"Yes, Les, but only a white one. I feel very much better today so I didn't bother to take a brown one. I don't want to get into the way of taking medicine unless it's really necessary. It's almost like taking drugs." Les looked as though he wanted to say something, then changed his mind.

"When is the doctor coming again?" I asked.

"Tomorrow. He said he'll give me another injection, but I think I'll ask him not to. I'm sure I don't need one and he wouldn't say what it's for."

"For God's sake, woman," burst out Les, "when you find a good doctor who suits you, why can't you trust him and just do what he says?" But Amy wasn't paying attention.

"Come along, dears," she called, waving a hand to the three children who were wandering up the path, "come along, you're just in time for morning tea."

"They always are," I said. "They can hear the rattle of a biscuit tin half a mile away." The youngest, a chubby blue-eyed little boy with fair curly hair, came running first.

"Nanna, I want a drink a milk."

"Yes, dear, but what do you say?"

"Please, Nanna," he caught sight of the plate of biscuits, "I want a chocklit biscuit."

"Me too," cried his big sister, "one for me too, Nanna."

"And how about you, Margaret? Would you like something to eat, dear?"

"Yes, please, Mrs Perfect," said the little fair girl from next door. She came forward shyly, holding a big cardboard box under her arm.

"Why, Margaret, whatever have you got there? Don't tell me it's a present from Father Christmas."

"Father Kwismis," echoed the little boy, looking nervously over his shoulder, and he scrambled over to me and buried his face in my lap.

"Yes, Mrs Perfect, and it's just what I asked him to leave me, a walkie-talkie doll, and I'm going to call it Suzanne."

"And it *really* talks, Nanna, and if you hold its hand the right way it walks along too, just like a toddler, just like John," shouted the sister, jumping up and down with excitement.

"John's *not* a toddler," roared the small one, leaving my lap and turning pink with rage, "John's a *nice boy.*"

"No, you're not, you're just a toddler." The nice boy burst into tears and stamped with frustration.

"Now, stop it you two," said Amy. "And, Margaret, do take the lid off, I'm just dying to see Suzanne." The child stood on one wobbly leg, balanced the box precariously on the other raised knee and slowly removed the lid.

"Oh, Margaret, isn't she beautiful, isn't she the biggest doll ever, and just look at her clothes," breathed Amy, lifting Suzanne out of the box. She certainly was the most expensive-looking doll I had ever seen. Expense was written all over her yellow straw hat trimmed with pink rosebuds, and her frilly nylon dress held out by stiffened petticoats, and the gleaming black patent leather shoes with silver buckles.

"Wouldn't have one on my mind," muttered Les. "You can't expect kids to keep a thing like that intact. The slightest thing throws them out of gear, and then they're finished, done for. And there's all your money down the drain."

"Yes," I agreed, "but you must admit that this one is a real beauty. You can't blame the kids for wanting it, I wouldn't mind having it myself." The toddler had stopped dead in his tracks, completely overawed by the beautiful toy that stood nearly as high as himself.

"Come here, John," said Amy quietly. "Come and see Suzanne. Isn't she a pretty big dolly? Wouldn't you like to hold her hand?" The little boy went up to the doll slowly, right up till he was nearly touching her.

"She got a hat on, Nanna?"

"Yes, John, and look at the pretty flowers on it." He lifted the dress up suddenly and peered underneath.

"She got panties on, Nanna?"

"Yes, dear, she's got on real panties, just like a little girl." He stared into the blue glass eyes for a long moment, then put his arms round the doll and drew her to him and kissed her carefully on the mouth.

"No, John, no," shrieked his sister, "you mustn't do that, you naughty boy, you'll make her face all dirty." And she sprang forward and tried to pull the doll out of his arms. There was a struggling heap of doll and toddler and little girls for a few seconds till Amy managed to disengage them and lifted Suzanne on to the safety of her lap.

"Now listen to me children," she said, gasping slightly. "Father Christmas would be hurt if you were to break Suzanne, because she is one of his very special toys, and she takes a long time to make. You know how careful you have to be with a baby? Well, a walkie-talkie is so special it's almost like a baby and you have to take just as much care of her. So remember, be good and kind to your dollies and look after them and love them because they won't last for ever. Will they?" She looked straight across at me.

"No," I shook my head, making ready to support her argument, and then something in her look made me stop and I forgot all about the doll and the children.

"There, Suzanne, you're quite all right now, aren't you?" and she smoothed down the golden hair and straightened the little straw hat. "My word, that nearly frightened the life out of you, didn't it?" She smiled down at the doll on her knee. And then she leaned forward and lowered Suzanne slowly, carefully into the nest of pink tissue paper lining the box.

"Ashes to ashes, and dust to dust," she murmured, so quietly, I wondered if I had heard aright. The waxen lids drooped, hiding the vacant blue eyes from the sun.

"Amy, for God's sake, what are you saying?" whispered Les in a voice harsh with shock, and he half rose to his feet, the muscles of his face drawn tight with lines of strain and anxiety.

"Let me give you another cup of tea, dear," Amy said calmly, holding out her hand. For a full minute they stared at each other, Les struggling to deny the meaning in his wife's eyes, then he passed his cup over without a word and sank back on the step, his hands hanging limply between his knees and his head turned away from the box at his feet. But the little boy crouched down on his haunches beside it and stared curiously at the doll.

"She gone asleep, Nanna, she gone a bye-bye?"

"Yes, dear, shsh, don't wake her up, she's very very tired, let her have a nice long sleep now." The child reached out a finger and touched one plastic hand gently. Then he tiptoed down the path after the others, his curly head hunched between his shoulders.

I got up and went back inside to the sitting-room. Everything looked the same in the small neat room, clean and shining and fresh with flowers. Everything was in order. Everything was ready. And tomorrow the doctor would come, and again next week, and again and again, all through the weary summer, till the heat lost its strength and could hold on no longer, and gave way to autumn at last, and the long night of winter. Another gust of wind sprang unnoticed upon the house and swept its way through with noisy movement, like panic sweeping through a crowd. I turned full circle before it and grabbed blindly at another paperback.

"When they were all fixed in a state of suspended animation Hunt set the chronometer control to free them a dozen centuries ahead. Then he settled himself in the last cubicle and swung the headpiece into position. As his hand reached to throw the master switch, he paused a moment. Would they find what they wanted on the first awakening? Or would their search take them through countless awakenings into Eternity?"

But the image of a big golden-haired doll laid out in pink tissue paper blurred the print till the words were meaningless.

The Too Good Memsahib

"*So let us heed this clarion call, not to arms and antagonism, but to a sustained and determined assault upon the barriers which still exist between the East and the West.*" The memsahib reread the last sentence of her article, 'The Changing Role of the European in the East Today', and leaned back in her chair with a sigh of satisfaction. Not bad, not bad at all. No world shaker but maybe strong enough to shake a few false beliefs like the old 'East is East, and West is West' and the more up to date, 'they are born to suffering and hardship and aren't affected by them as we would be given the same circumstances'. Easy to build effective barriers out of that kind of talk, and easier still to believe them insurmountable because then there was no point in bothering about what was happening on the other side. Well, she'd taken a jolly good swing at that one, and at some of the people back home too, who were busy growing ulcers over a better job-house-car-fridge-radiogram-spindryer success with security, what to do with aged parents, and their own unavoidable deaths; when three weeks travelling nor'west would land them among millions who spent their lives struggling to keep alive without the barest necessities. Not that the people back home weren't generous. Look at the tons of old clothes they gave to Corso every year and money too, and dried milk to Indonesia, and stamps for the lepers, and hadn't they largely financed a new hospital here in Delhi, or was it a milk department in Bombay? No, their hearts were all right, if you knew how to touch them, but it was very much a case of 'what the eye doesn't see' with them. She wondered what would happen if they were all suddenly dumped, the two and a half million of them, in the middle of Calcutta. Would their eyes and ears fly open for ever, hands ache to give till there was nothing left, hearts crack because it wasn't nearly enough, or would complacency win the day? Odd that such a discontented people could be so complacent. That is why she had been at such pains to paint a vivid picture of what she had seen. She flicked over the pages of manuscript. Yes, here it was — people sleeping on the streets, armies of beggars waiting outside the churches, children sold into 'service' for a few rupees — a bit highly coloured perhaps, but the sort of stuff that the reading public back home were used to and understood. She sighed again for her countrymen who didn't know they were alive, and was reaching out a hand to the bowl of fruit in the middle of the table, when she heard the crash. She selected an orange, wondering idly what the noise was this time. It had taken her quite a while to become accustomed to the unfamiliar sounds which besieged the house night and day — food vendors' calls so melancholy they could have been offering the world's grief for a few annas instead of bananas and fish and icecream; quavering arias from a couple of scantily clad beggars supporting each other as they paraded painfully in front of the square white bungalows; a drummer drumming as only an Indian can, before a procession advertising the coming attraction at the local cinema; nightwatchmen calling to each other with long up-rising unnerving cries choked on a gasp as they patrolled the badly lit streets; and in the wakeful small hours light winds stirred through nearby empty tombs and came whispering, whispering down alleyways and along walls and under doors of dust and death and long-gone Mogul kings. But this noise was harshly different, as though someone had dragged and pushed a very heavy metal object along the road, something like an enormous tin trunk or an upturned car ....

The memsahib dropped the half-peeled orange and hurried to the windows facing the street, and as she peered through the gauze screens two stout Indian women scurried past the wall, hands clutching at saris slipping from their heads. Without thinking what she was doing, the memsahib was out the front door, across the porch and down the steps and leaning over the gate. The two women had disappeared and the narrow tree-lined street was curiously quiet and deserted except for a small black taxi standing in the middle of the road a couple of doors away. The memsahib pushed through the gate uncertainly, and then she saw the boy. He was dragging himself painfully from under the back of the car, and as he staggered to his feet, she ran, but didn't quite catch him as he slumped backwards as though from a blow to the jaw. The memsahib swallowed hard with fear as she squatted beside him and saw the long deep gash running up his forehead into his hair, and the slack limbs spread wide. My god, he was dead, no, eyelids flickering, dying then. She caught his hand desperately, and called him poor boy, good boy in faltering Hindi, but the blank eyes didn't seem to focus on her, and she couldn't understand what he was trying to whimper. Still, he could whimper. She looked down the slight body again and could see no other wounds except deep grazes, but did not dare move him in case of internal injuries. She stroked his cheek and murmured, "I'll be right back. Don't worry," gave him a brilliant reassuring smile in case he didn't understand English, and sped back to the house, shouting for their cook-bearer, Ram Srup, who was preparing lunch in the kitchen.

"Come quickly, there's been an accident outside and I need your help," she gasped breathless at the door. Ram Srup stared at her a moment, put his knife down deliberately on the chopping board, and began fiddling with the apron strings behind his back. The memsahib fairly danced with impatience and shook him by the arm.

"Never mind about that, come *now*, I tell you it's urgent," and she turned and ran, leaving him to follow. A small group of poorly dressed Indians were milling around the boy, shoving and shouting at each other, and she paused a moment, wondering where they had all come from so quickly (certainly not from the bungalows), or had they been watching her with the child all the time, and hanging back till she went, and if so, why? She was trying to come at the boy when a small thin woman with wild eyes pushed past her frantically and fell on him with a piercing scream. His mother, guessed the memsahib, as the wailing woman rocked to and fro on her haunches, her face contorted with pain and fear, but pity soon gave way to a slight irritation as the rocking and wailing persisted. I wish she'd shut up, thought the memsahib, it's enough to convince the child he's really dying. And then, abruptly, the racket did stop. Everyone was still in the sudden quiet, and the memsahib watched, puzzled at first, then unbelievingly, as the woman, with an intent look on her face, slipped a crooked finger into the boy's mouth, hooked out a rupee piece, and tied it swiftly in a corner of her sari. The next moment pandemonium broke loose. The mother, shrieking worse than ever, seized the boy by his shoulders and tried to shake him into a sitting position, while two other women hauled at his arms, and a man tried to lift him by the legs. The memsahib watched with horror as the moaning twisting child was pulled this way and that, and then she was pushing and shouting with the rest of them.

"You'll kill him, you fools, you'll kill him. Put him down, I tell you, leave him alone. Get back — back." She tore the women's hands away and hauled

THE TOO GOOD MEMSAHIB

the hysterical mother to one side, not too gently, and straddled the boy.

"Now," she said in a loud clear voice, drawing herself up to full height and looking around, "taxi driver, is the taxi driver here?" A tall elderly Sikh with a grey beard who had been hovering in the background nodded his head dumbly. "Right. You will take us to the hospital. Hospital, understand? Get in the car." She faced the crowd again. "Now, is father here? Father, father," and she pointed down at the boy. Two men stepped forward at once. "Which, father?" she asked, looking at each in turn, but they only stared blankly at one another. "Never mind. Lift the boy up and put him in the back seat of the taxi," and she went through actions to show what she meant. The mother started forward, her face working, as she saw her child being taken away, but the memsahib held her back by the arm, saying, "I'm sorry, he must go to hospital immediately. Don't worry, I'll look after him." But the woman shook her hand off and stepped back with a dark look, and stood glowering and gnawing at her knuckles. The memsahib slammed the back door of the taxi on the two men awkwardly nursing the boy, and got into the front seat herself with enormous relief. Just as the Sikh started the car, Ram Srup came running towards them from the direction of the market, waving his arms to them to wait. Another man followed close behind.

"A doctor, memsahib, a doctor," he panted. She got out of the car reluctantly, opened the back door again, and watched as the man examined the wound and felt over the scalp. The boy winced and began to whimper.

"Should he go to hospital?" The man nodded as he ran his hands over the limbs.

"Yes, immediately," he said, straightening up, "that needs stitching, and he should have an x-ray and anti-tetanus. Also examined for internal injuries. Are you taking him?"

"Yes, of course," replied the memsahib, "I think Okhla is …" she stopped as the man shook his head.

"No use going there, they won't treat him."

"Why not?" But he only shrugged and fluttered his hands, fingers spread wide in a popular gesture she had come to dislike. It could mean anything as long as it was negative.

"Look," she insisted, "I'm sure they'll take him. The Indian doctor there is a very close friend of mine, and I know she won't turn us away." The man raised his eyebrows sceptically.

"All right. You can try," and he slammed the door. The mother sprang at the car as they moved off, and tried to keep level with the back window. Before they turned the corner the memsahib looked back, and saw her standing in the middle of the road, clutching her head in her hands, and given over completely to loud grief.

"Do you know the way to Okhla hospital?" asked the memsahib, turning to the driver. He nodded, without taking his eyes off the road.

She felt a little uneasy. Did he understand English and was just too upset to say a word, or was he only pretending to understand? That kind of pretending could lead to all kinds of trouble, as she had learnt to her cost.

"Well, go as fast as you can, but be careful of potholes. The boy shouldn't be jolted." He immediately put his foot down on the accelerator and the memsahib sat back satisfied — he did understand. But once on the main road the stream of motley traffic slowed them down. Bicycles, with what seemed whole families clinging to them, wobbled precariously among pedestrians in the thick orange dust at the side of the tarseal. Slow clumsy bullock carts, often loaded with heavy logs that stuck out dangerously at all angles, gave way to no one, except perhaps the ramshackle wooden trucks, driven by grinning madmen who threatened the lives of everyone near and far. Light open carriages carrying people who hadn't been able to force their way into the overflowing buses, were drawn by miserable looking horses decked out in bright bobbles and cockades. And weaving their way through it all went the scooters or auto-rickshaws, like outsize motor cycles with canopied seats bouncing behind. As a rule the memsahib was fascinated by all this, and the shabby wayside markets thronged with people, and the whitewashed hutments alive with children too poor to go to school, and the fine new embankment, built, as far as she could make out, by one ridiculously small steamroller and an endless stream of women balancing wide shallow baskets of soil on their heads like hats. And then the open fields of waving grain, green and gold and deceptively empty. But today she fidgeted in her seat, one eye on the speedometer and the other on the boy, who whimpered as he held his head and tried to keep the blood out of his eyes and mouth. At last they turned into a side road, and there, standing square and uncompromising in a stony field, as though it had been left high and dry by some all-powerful flood, stood the hospital. More like a fortress against expected attack than a place of healing, thought the memsahib gloomily, but the inside was different, cool and light and spacious, with more than a hint of sound financial foundations, and entirely lacking the makeshift atmosphere that depressed so many Indian public offices. For this was a private institution, controlled and partly staffed by 'foreigners' who built with an eye to the future (no doubt the Mogul kings had done the same), and could afford to insist that air-conditioning was a necessity, not a luxury. The memsahib felt more cheerful as they ground round the heavily metalled drive, past the front entrance flanked by potted shrubs, to the Outpatients and Casualty wards at the side. Their arrival caused quite a stir in the large well-appointed waiting-room, almost, thought the memsahib uneasily, as though they weren't used to admitting accident cases. The receptionist looked flustered, and an Indian nurse in stiff incredibly white gown and headgear hurried forward nervously with a steel wheelchair.

"Just a minute," she said, backing away from them, "and I'll tell doctor you are here," but the memsahib followed her into the surgery, and there was Dru, a little unfamiliar with a white coat and an air of authority. She waved her patient to one side and came forward immediately when she saw the memsahib behind the nurse.

"My dear, what brings you here? Is there trouble? Where are the children?" The memsahib began talking excitedly, greatly relieved to be pouring the story into an understanding ear, while Dru listened gravely without a word.

"Bring him in and I'll examine him." The boy looked alarmingly frail laid out on the high white couch, but the memsahib felt reassured as she watched Dru's thin brown hands go to work, firm and gentle and confident. One of the best surgeons in Delhi, so she'd been told.

"Limbs are all right except for deep grazing," said Dru at last, "but this will have to be stitched, and he should have x-rays and be kept under observation for concussion." The memsahib nodded.

"That's just what the doctor from the market said."

"That means he will have to be admitted. Do you wish to do so?"

"Of course, if it's necessary," answered the memsahib, surprised.

"It means signing a form and taking responsibility in place of his parent."

"That's all right, I'll sign anything, so long as he gets the treatment he needs." Dru gave her a long look.

"Very well, I'll attend to the wound first. It might be better if you wait outside. Then we'll see about the admission form. And don't worry, he'll be all right now." The memsahib found a seat near the door and looked about her with interest. There seemed to be a dispensary at the far end of the room where a group of Indians, mainly old men and young mothers with babies, and all obviously poor, waited patiently on forms till the nurse behind the counter called them up for their prescriptions. The memsahib had heard, but not from the doctor herself, that most of Dru's salary was spent on her patients, though you wouldn't have suspected it from her aloof, almost indifferent manner. And hadn't she been just a little too formal and professional about the boy? After all, they were close friends. She hadn't asked a question or passed any comment about the accident or the memsahib's part in it, not that she was looking for a pat on the back or anything like that, still — but it didn't matter. She looked up as the nervous nurse came out of the surgery and rustled importantly out of sight. No, nothing mattered, as long as the boy was fixed up and not left lying neglected somewhere, and she was staying with him until he was.

Her mind went back to one Sunday afternoon last winter, when an English friend with two children had called in her car and taken them all out for a drive and picnic. New Delhi, and later the fringes of old Delhi, were familiar ground so they had crossed the Jumna bridge — a grimly impressive doubledecker structure with trains above and anything else below and guards at both ends — and made for the open country. Hardly clear of the bridge, they had found themselves in a queue being directed by traffic officers round the scene of an accident. They had been forced to crawl past a truck lying on its side, two dead bullocks sprawled under their yokes, an overturned cart and a jumble of logs as long as telegraph poles, a dead man with a dirty handkerchief over his face, and a completely wrecked scooter. It appeared the truck had passed the bullock cart too close and too fast from the opposite direction, and struck some of the logs protruding from the sides. Both vehicles had tipped away from each other, the cart dragging the bullocks down, and some of the logs which were sent flying in all directions smashed into a scooter following close behind and killed the driver. With oohs and aahs from the children and appropriate remarks from the adults, they had continued on their way, through a large village, past a Hindu temple, until they found themselves among bare fields.

Here they had stopped and made a picnic, the memsahib and her family nibbling with secret delight at the hostess's imported cheese and marmite sandwiches, both worth their weight in rupees, while the English woman watched doubtfully as her two children gobbled up the memsahib's thick peanut butter and lettuce sandwiches, both local products and therefore suspect. They had turned their backs on several Indians who were watching them from the road with undue interest and curiosity (it didn't occur to the memsahib till some time later that they might have been the owners of the field), and had talked like exiles of Home.

"I wish we were having a picnic in our very own woods," lisped the youngest English child wistfully, and her mother described their weekend cottage in some historic hamlet with an ancient Norman church near the Downs by the sea — the very heart of England surely. The memsahib's children conjured up picnics on Maori pa sites overlooking wild deserted beaches, or beside cold amber streams in mysterious bush thick with kiwis and pigeons, and the memsahib, a little awed by so much marmite and cheese, spoke apologetically of her native land which was really only three small islands on the map, rather near the South Pole, and she wasn't sure, but she thought there were more sheep than people. After they had packed the leftovers into the baskets the English woman produced toy fishing nets on long poles, and they had dragged them through the shallow weed-covered ditches bordering the field, till wonder of wonders, the memsahib caught a fish as long as her thumb, to the huge amusement of their Indian audience, and the little English girl stepped into the ditch in her excitement and was rather smelly afterwards. Then suddenly the warmth had gone out of the weak winter sun, and the children were made to put on jerseys and bundled into the car (chills always affected their bowels) and they drove back leisurely the way they had come a couple of hours ago, and there was the queue and the traffic officers directing them round a wrecked scooter, a corpse, a jumble of logs, two dead bullocks, and a cart and truck lying on their sides. Even the children were silent until they were across the bridge, and when the English woman offered to stop at Mahatma Gandhi's memorial, the memsahib had said wasn't it getting rather cold, perhaps another day, but thank you, thank you so much, it's been a lovely afternoon.

The memsahib came out of her memory with a start. The nurse was back again, looking more nervous than ever, and carrying a stainless steel tray with a white cloth thrown over various objects. Close on her heels came the first European the memsahib had seen since she left home, a large plump jolly sister, who crossed the room with long easy strides in spite of her gown, and had a little smile for everyone, including the memsahib, who took an intense dislike to her on the spot. She felt vaguely alarmed as the surgery door closed behind the pair. Had Dru come up against some complication and sent for the sister's help, and if so, why didn't they come out and tell her? She went to the door and was about to knock when it opened and the sister faced her, still with the little smile on her lips, but the memsahib noticed that the alert blue eyes were not at all amused.

"Ah, I think you're the lady I'm looking for," said the sister, proclaiming her nationality with every syllable. "Are you our doctor's friend who brought in the boy with the head injury?"

"Yes, I am," replied the memsahib quickly, "is he all right, or have you discovered something else wrong with him?"

"Oh no, nothing like that, he'll be a box of birds in a day or two," she sounded almost gay, "after one or two little jobs have been attended to. But I'm afraid we can't do it here, he'll have to go somewhere else." The little smile became rueful as she shook her head gently. The memsahib blinked as though she had been flicked across the eyes, and couldn't believe that she had heard correctly.

"Did you say …" she faltered, "I'm afraid I don't understand." The sister dropped her voice confidingly.

"You see, we are terribly understaffed here, and we simply can't allow our doctor time off to appear in court. We would have to send all these people away, and many others, just for the sake of one boy."

"Appear in court?" repeated the memsahib foolishly. What on earth was the woman babbling about? The sister smiled patiently and went on.

"The boy obviously comes from a poor family, and his parents, if he has any, are bound to try and make money out of this. They'll probably sue the taxi company for several hundred rupees, and if we admit him, we'll be called upon …" But the memsahib wasn't listening. Out of the corner of her eye she could see the doctor hovering unhappily in the background, and she was recalling one or two remarks Dru had let slip about her position in the hospital and the treatment of the Indian staff. She hadn't paid much attention at the time, dismissing it as ordinary grumbling about work which everyone indulged in now and again, but suddenly the whole set-up was painfully clear. Poor Dru. And here she had unwittingly provided this smiling monster with a golden opportunity to over-ride Dru's authority publicly.

"I see," she said slowly, though in her anger she had missed the point of the sister's argument. The sister gave a delighted smile but the memsahib ignored it and went on.

"It was a mistake to consider coming here at all. As a matter of fact, if it hadn't been for your doctor's excellent reputation, I wouldn't have." The smile faded a little. Ah, how she would have enjoyed wiping it off altogether. "And what do you suggest I do with the boy?"

"Well, you could take him back to where you found him," said the sister watching her carefully, but the memsahib wasn't to be drawn for Dru's sake, "or you could send him to the nearest public hospital."

"I'll take him, not send him," put in the memsahib sharply. The sister shrugged slightly.

"In that case, I'm sure doctor can direct you better than I. But it's not at all necessary for you to go. This is only a minor accident, and these people are used to looking after themselves. Good morning." Dru beckoned the memsahib into the surgery as soon as the sister had turned her back on them. Her professional manner was quite gone.

"I'm sorry," she began miserably, "but you see what it's like. They take no notice of what I say. They give the orders and I do the work." The memsahib nodded sympathetically, but didn't trust herself to say what she was feeling. She shook Dru gently by the arm.

"It doesn't matter. Don't worry about me, I'm not the least bit hurt or offended, but tell me what to do with the boy. The sister said take him to the nearest public hospital. Where's that?"

"At Safderjung, a suburb about half an hour's drive from here, but the taxi driver will know the way. There's no need for you to go. Why don't you get them to take you home first? It won't take long. That's what I would do if I were you." But the memsahib looked down with a frown and shook her head. This was certainly not the time or place to open a discussion about the role of the foreigner and breaking barriers.

"Dru, I won't be satisfied until I see the boy safe and sound in some hospital. I'll let you know what happens. And do come and see us as soon as you can get away from the ugly sister."

The memsahib was silent as they swung round the drive again and headed back the way they had come. Rushing into the arms of a capable and reliable friend was one thing, but casting oneself upon the mercy of unknown Indian officials was quite another matter, and the prospect secretly dismayed her. Her heart sank still further as she remembered her one and only visit to a public hospital with an Indian friend. The place was a maze of long one-storeyed wings arranged in adjoining squares, and they had wandered up and down gloomy concrete corridors with barred gauze windows on one side and even gloomier and unbearably stuffy wards opening off the other.

Small groups of relatives clustered round the doors waiting for death or discharge, it was hard to tell which, but several squatting outside the operating theatre were weeping openly. The friend had had enormous difficulty in finding the patient she had come to visit. He had apparently been moved to another ward, but no one knew where or when or why. The hollow-eyed nurses seemed too stupid with tiredness to even understand what they wanted, while the sisters were too busy to be bothered or even civil when pressed for directions. In the end they had stopped asking questions and found him only by going through the wards one by one. If that kind of thing could happen to an Indian who spoke and understood the language, what could happen to her with her half dozen Hindi words badly pronounced? She was beginning to realise that the language barrier was much more difficult to overcome than she had suggested in her article. And how it set one at a disadvantage. She would very much like to know, for instance, what those two in the back seat were whispering to each other, and why the driver started when they touched him on the shoulder and said something in rapid Hindi. The memsahib looked at him closely.

"You are taking us to Safderjung, aren't you?" He nodded briefly. "Then why are we nearly back to where we started?" asked the memsahib, glancing out the window. "Do we have to come this way?" He nodded again as they slowed down past the market, and with that drew up outside the suburban police station. The memsahib looked out with alarm. A group of police officers in khaki shorts and shirts and cockaded turbans were watching them from the porch, and two of them hurried forward as the car stopped.

"What's this, why are you stopping here?" said the memsahib, turning first to the driver, then to the men in the back seat, but they ignored her and said something instead to the policeman peering into the car. The memsahib let down her window with a bang.

"What do you want?" she asked him curtly. "We're in a hurry. This boy has been hurt and we're taking him to Safderjung hospital." The man smiled and nodded.

"I know, memsahib, but we wish to make out a report of the accident. Will you please bring the boy inside?"

"Can't it wait till we've taken him to hospital? I promise you we'll all come straight back here." He smiled again, shaking his head, and opened the back door. The man nursing the boy began to clamber out awkwardly, but caught the boy's head on the edge of the door, and a thin trickle of blood showed below the rough bandage Dru had put on hastily before they left her. The memsahib pulled him back in the seat and turned on the policeman, her eyes blazing, and voice shaking with anger.

"See what you've done," she stormed, "you've made it bleed again. I tell you, this is an urgent case. He needs stitching and injections and x-rays immediately. And you want us to stop for a silly report."

"Now then, memsahib," warned the officer, his smile gone, "be careful what you say." But the memsahib turned her back on him and shouted in the driver's frightened face.

"Drive on, damn you, take no notice of these fools, drive to Safderjung *now*." As the car shot forward, the second policeman grabbed at the swinging door and half jumped, half fell into the back seat on top of the others. The memsahib glared at him without a word as he tried to squeeze himself into the corner. Well, if he wanted a ride they'd take him for one, to Safderjung and nowhere else. But after a few minute's strained silence, the memsahib began to feel uncomfortable and a little sheepish. After all, the man was a policeman and only doing his duty, and perhaps this time she had jumped one barrier too many. Anyway, it was too ridiculous behaving as though the other didn't exist. She turned round with an effort and asked, "Do you understand English?"

There was a long pause while the man stared at her coldly. "Memsahib," he replied finally, with great deliberation, "I cannot speak a word of English."

"Oh," said the memsahib, turning to the front again quickly. That was a slap in the face and no mistake, but if he thought it would shut her up for good, leaving him in control of the situation, he couldn't be more wrong. She tried again.

"Please tell me, how long will it take us to reach Safderjung?" There was an even longer pause, and the memsahib was steeling herself to repeat the question, when the man mumbled grudgingly, almost under his breath,

"Ten minutes from the police station." The memsahib beamed on him.

"Oh good. It's not as far as I thought. That means we're nearly there. Thank you very much." She was trying to think up more questions to keep the conversation going when the driver swung the car across the road, through an open gateway, and pulled up before a long low whitewashed building. They lifted the boy out carefully and followed the policeman past the padlocked front entrance round to the back and along a verandah. A man, who could have been a porter, stood up leisurely as they approached, and waved them through a swinging gauze door. They found themselves in a small dark room without windows, a high couch against one wall, a washbasin against the other, and open doorways leading off right and left. There was no electric fan. It must be unbearable in the summer, thought the memsahib, but then electric fans were as much a luxury for the Indians as air-conditioners were for the Europeans. A man in a white coat was carrying on an animated telephone conversation at a desk in the middle of the floor. A young nurse — are all Indian nurses hollow-eyed, wondered the memsahib — was rolling bandages behind him. Another man in a white coat hurried across the floor with a bunch of thin rubber tubes dangling in his hand. No one took the slightest notice of them as they hesitated inside the door. At last the policeman whispered to the man carrying the boy, and they tiptoed across the room and laid him on the couch. The memsahib, who was feeling extremely uncomfortable and nervous, followed and took up a defensive stand beside him.

"Memsahib," he whispered, and she bent down anxiously, all ears. "Pani, pani," and he slowly carried one cupped hand to his lips. She turned quickly to the nurse.

"The boy is asking for a drink of water. Will you fetch him one, please?" The nurse glanced at her briefly and waved one hand towards the washbasin.

"But there's no tumbler," said the memsahib sharply. The nurse looked her up and down with narrowed hostile eyes, and pointed to a pink plastic beaker no bigger than an eggcup. The memsahib flushed and was about to say something unbecoming to a barrier-breaker when she became aware that the man at the desk had finished his conversation and was watching her closely.

"Yes?" he said, as she caught his stare. "What is the trouble?" He spoke clipped precise English, a shade too quickly.

"This boy was run over by a car. We took him to Okhla hospital but they advised us to bring him here." The man nodded without surprise.

"The doctor there examined him and said he needs stitches and x-rays ..." The man cut her short with a wave of his hand.

"It was your car that ran over him?"

"No, it wasn't my car, it was a taxi."

"I see. And you were in the taxi?"

"No, I wasn't in the taxi." What was he getting at? The man said something to the policeman in Hindi, who nodded and gestured to the driver behind him. The man leaned back in his seat and looked at the memsahib curiously.

"Then how did you come to pick him up and take him to hospital?"

"The accident occurred outside my front gate, and I was the first on the scene. When his friends and relatives came they didn't seem to know what to do, so I …" she hesitated as the man smiled slowly.

"So you stepped in and decided for them." His expression changed abruptly. "Do you wish to admit him?" The memsahib nodded.

"Then sign here, please," and he pushed a pen and paper across the desk.

"Thank you, that will be all."

"But I didn't finish telling you what the doctor said at Okhla," protested the memsahib.

"There's no need to," he replied shortly, "we will give him whatever treatment is necessary after we have examined him." He stood up as though the interview had come to an end, but the memsahib made one last desperate effort.

"Will you keep him waiting long? It must be nearly two hours since …" but he interrupted her irritably.

"Madam, this is only a minor accident, and he will have to wait his turn. We have admitted three accident cases this morning, all serious, the last one just before you came. Look." The memsahib glanced in the direction he nodded, through the open doorway, where the man with the rubber tubes had disappeared. She caught a glimpse of two bare feet protruding from what seemed to be a bundle of stained rags dumped on a couch, and looked away quickly.

"Your boy is our fourth case, and we will have as many again before the day is through." The memsahib noticed for the first time how drawn and strained his face was in spite of its mask of efficiency.

"And if they are all more serious than the boy?" she asked, knowing what the answer would be. "Then I suppose there's no point in waiting any longer?"

"No, none at all. Good morning." The memsahib said goodbye to the boy as cheerfully as she could — one of the men who had carried him in had given him a drink from the beaker — patted his hand and hurried outside, almost weeping with frustration and despair. The policeman was waiting for her.

"I'm going home now," she told him in a dull flat voice.

"Home," he exclaimed, starting back in mock surprise. "But what about the boy? Are you going to leave him alone?" The memsahib suddenly felt very tired. Oh, to be safe in her own place, and quit of these people for ever.

"I can't do any more," she said quietly, "and he's in good hands. There's no point in hanging around here, and besides, I have children coming home from school." The man smiled down at her as she spoke, openly enjoying his little victory, but the memsahib was past caring.

"Where is the taxi driver?" she asked, looking round. "I'll get him to drive me home." The policeman frowned and shook his head.

"Why not?" she protested.

"Because he's under arrest."

"But how am I going to get back? I can't walk." She felt as though she were struggling in a nightmare.

"You will find a scooter stand round the corner," he said stiffly. The memsahib stared at him unbelievingly.

"Do you mean to say, that after all I've done this morning, you are now telling me I can take myself off in a scooter, and pay my own fare too, I suppose?" She felt a brief return of her old spirit. "Well, I'm not. I'm going home in that taxi, and I want to go now." The man looked slightly apprehensive as her voice rose. She meant what she said, and he knew it, but he tried to reason with her.

"You don't understand, memsahib, this man is in trouble, and if I let him go he will try to run away, and if you are with him, he'll take you too." But the memsahib only laughed.

"Don't be silly. He's a good man, you can see it in his face. He was so upset about the boy I'm sure he won't dream of running away." She pressed her attack as the policeman wavered. "I'll tell you what I'll do. I'll get him to drive me to the police station, hand him over to your sergeant, and then walk home from there. And if anything goes wrong, I'll take the responsibility." While the policeman was trying to think up some objection to this scheme, besides the perfectly adequate one he had already raised, the memsahib backed away, whisked round the corner into the taxi, and was off.

"Take me back to the police station, please," she said pleasantly, looking hard at the man's profile. It *was* a good face. She decided to risk telling him the truth.

"I'm afraid the policeman told me I was to hand you over to the sergeant at the station. I'm sorry, but it has to be done. It will only mean more trouble for you if I don't. Do you understand?" The man nodded miserably, and in ten minutes they were there. The policemen were still on the porch, and hurried forward to open the door when the memsahib beckoned to them through the window.

"Thank you," she said meekly, rather enjoying their puzzled looks as she got out. "Your man cannot leave the hospital yet, and he asked me to hand the taxi driver over to you on my way home. So here he is. Good morning." The sergeant collected himself with an effort and managed to return her pleasant smile, before she turned her back on him and made for home.

Ram Srup greeted her dramatically at the front door.

"Ah, memsahib, it is you. The boy … will he live? All morning I pray that he will live." He joined his hands together and rolled his eyes. The memsahib nodded.

"He'll be all right. I took him to hospital." Ram Srup made a small salaam.

"The memsahib is too good, too good. One day she will surely go to heaven," and he rolled his eyes again, and drew a circle in the air above his head. The memsahib bit her lip with embarrassment and vexation. She had often wished that Ram Srup, who was a prizewinning product of a missionary compound, would keep his confounded religious beliefs to himself. If he hadn't been such a good cook he would have prayed himself out of the job long ago. The family were finishing lunch and clamoured for news as she took her place at table.

"I'll give you the details later," she murmured to her husband. "It's been a morning."

"I bet it has," he said, getting up. "I've got an appointment at two-thirty, but I'll be back as soon as I can and hear all about it then."

He patted her on the shoulder and went.

"Go on, Mummy, tell us," began her small son, wriggling with impatience. "Ram Srup said you were looking after a boy who got hurt. What happened to him?"

"A taxi ran over the top of him," replied the memsahib, helping herself to fish pie.

"Gee — is he dead?" The memsahib shook her head at two pairs of wide eyes.

"I bet there was a lot of blood, though. What did you do with him?"

"Put him in the taxi and took him to hospital. His head had to be stitched up."

"I bet he didn't want to go. Did he cry?"

"No, he was a very brave boy."

"Was his mother or father there?" put in the girl.

"His mother was," said the memsahib, reaching for the date scones and butter.

"I bet she was worried. Did she go in the taxi too?"

"I know," chimed in the boy, "the two of you picked him up like this, and the mother got in the back seat backwards and held his head, and you sat beside the driver and told him where to go."

"The mother didn't go to the hospital," said the memsahib, stirring her tea quickly.

"Why ever not?" gasped the girl. "Didn't she want to?"

"Yes, but I wouldn't take her. She was crying and screaming and making an awful fuss." There was a shocked silence, and the memsahib could feel the children staring at her as she drank her tea. She put the cup down with a clatter and pushed it away.

"Now hurry up if you've finished your lunch, and get your books out. Let's do your homework right away and get it over."

"But mummy," hesitated the girl with a troubled look, "do you think you should have stopped the mother from going?"

"Whew," whistled the boy, "fancy going to hospital without your mother and having stitches." He screwed up his face and shivered.

"That's enough about it," said the memsahib sharply, getting up from the table. "The boy will be all right, that's the main thing. Now come over here and let me hear your three times first."

"Three noughts are nought, three ones are three, three twos are six — Mummy," broke in the boy, "what is that policeman doing in our backyard?" The memsahib looked quickly over her shoulder through the open door that led to the next room, separated by gauze screens from the small concrete courtyard beyond. The policeman from the hospital was taking notes, while Ram Srup held forth with dramatic gestures and postures, as he played the role of witness to the crime. The policeman nodded his head as though satisfied, slipped the book into his breast pocket, and glancing slyly towards the house, said something which set them both shaking with silent laughter. The memsahib bent hurriedly over the book in her lap. Let them talk, let them laugh, let them do what they like. She had done what she wanted to do in spite of them all, and now the subject was closed as far as she was concerned.

"Go on, never mind about him, he looks like a friend of Ram Srup," she told the gaping children. "Where were you up to? Three twos are six, three threes are nine …"

But the subject wasn't quite closed. Early in the evening, just as dinner was being served, Ram Srup answered a ring at the front door and came back to announce solemnly that the boy's father wished to talk with the memsahib. She went out reluctantly, taking Ram Srup with her to act as interpreter if necessary, and was surprised to find a man she had never seen before, waiting on the front porch.

"There must be some mistake, Ram Srup. Are you sure he says he is the father?"

"Yes, memsahib."

"But I don't understand. He isn't either of the two men — never mind. What does he want?"

"He say, what have you done with his son?"

"What have I *done* with his son? Tell him, nothing, except take him to Safderjung hospital this morning."

"He say, why you do that?" The memsahib was becoming impatient.

"Good heavens, Ram Srup, doesn't he know about the accident? Tell him what happened, and hurry, the food will be cold." Ram Srup began to orate, but the man kept interrupting, and the next thing they were shouting at each other.

"Hello, what's up?" asked the memsahib's husband, coming into the hall. The man glared at them all, turned on his heel, and stumped angrily across the courtyard and out the gate. The memsahib watched him go in amazement.

"What on earth's the matter with him, Ram Srup? What was he saying?"

"I tell him *not* your car, *not* your taxi, and he say *not* your business then, and I tell him if my memsahib not been there, his boy surely die. Bad man, memsahib, bad man," and he went back to the kitchen shaking his head and muttering under his breath.

The memsahib was quiet and preoccupied during the meal, and after the children had been washed and put to bed, and Ram Srup had said goodnight with much ceremony and gone home, she took out her article and went over it for the last time.

"It's not bad, you know," she remarked to her husband cheerfully, "not bad at all. I had a few doubts about it this morning, but nothing serious." She turned back to the beginning and began numbering the pages. "What did you make of that man this evening?"

"What man?" asked her husband. "Oh, you mean father number three." He shook his newspaper with a snort. "Ridiculous bloke, and damned ungrateful too. Not your business indeed. It's a wonder Ram Srup didn't land him one."

"I'm not too sure about Ram Srup," said the memsahib slowly. "I have a sneaking feeling that he thoroughly enjoyed the whole affair. Yes, I thought the father was ridiculous too, but you know, I have another sneaking feeling that the doctor at Safderjung took pretty much the same attitude, not to mention that monster at Okhla. Almost as though I were interfering instead of going out of my way to be as helpful as I could. Even Dru wanted me to send the boy on by himself. That shook me a little." She stacked the typed sheets neatly and folded them to fit the long envelope. "There, that's done. Will you post it for me next time you go to town?" She yawned and stretched in her chair. "Lord, I'm tired, I think I'd better go to bed. Did I tell you about the washerwoman's little girl?" Her husband put aside his paper with a sigh.

"Not another sad story? Haven't you had enough?"

"No, not me," she smiled. "Well, I've discovered the child's got scabies on her scalp as well as lice, and I reckon her hair should be cut. The father says no, but I think I will all the same."

"Really, my dear," her husband protested, "do you think it's safe to play round with something like that? Isn't it catching?"

"Pooh," she said lightly, "people like us don't catch things like that. And then when I've got rid of the hair, I'll be able to give her head a good scrub with carbolic soap."

"What in?" asked the husband anxiously.

"Don't worry," she laughed, "I'll use the sweeper's bucket."

"But don't they look on the sweeper as untouchable? And I should think that would go for his bucket too."

"I've no idea," she yawned again, "and anyway if they do, it's time they didn't. So it looks as though I'm going to have another busy morning. Goodnight," she said at the door, "don't wear yourself out over that paper."

Her husband watched her go, with puzzled admiration, before turning back to his reading. She did some damn queer things at times, but she was a good woman, all right, and a good memsahib too.

First Native and Pink Pig

Mrs Harrison sat patiently at the kitchen table, pen poised above the last invitation, and looked across at her small son.

"Come on," she urged, "can't you make up your mind? Who's the last one going to be? And I wish you'd stop reading till we've finished this." George flopped his comic on the table with a sigh, folded his arms across it and reluctantly turned his attention on his mother.

"Can't I have both?"

"No, you can't," Mrs Harrison answered firmly, "we've been over all that before and the answer's still no." George screwed up his face.

"Well, I don't care which one I have. It doesn't matter much, does it?"

"As far as I'm concerned," said his mother, raising her eyebrows, "it doesn't matter at all, but I need a name to write on this. Which one is it going to be?"

"I don't know." Mrs Harrison put her pen down carefully and leaned back in her chair.

"Look, George, I've been sitting here for the last fifteen minutes waiting for you to make up your mind. Why can't you? What's holding you up? Can't you just say, I like Peter better than Michael — I'll have him, or Michael's good fun at a party — I'll have him? I can't see why you're finding it so difficult." George wriggled in his chair and fingered the comic.

"Well, I *do* like Peter better than Michael, but he gets asked to all the parties and Michael doesn't get asked to any."

"I see," Mrs Harrison said slowly. "Still, that doesn't mean you should ask Michael if you really don't want to. Any idea why he doesn't get asked?" George shrugged his shoulders.

"No, except that he's a bit rough with the little kids and gives a lot of cheek."

"Mmm, I don't like the sound of that. Anything else about him?" There was a long pause while George hunched himself over his comic.

"Yes," he muttered at last, "yes, there is. He doesn't like us." His mother

89

frowned in bewilderment and sat up straight in her chair.

"What do you mean, he doesn't like us? I've never met the child. How can he not like us if he doesn't even know us?" George crouched lower over the comic till his nose was nearly touching it.

"I don't mean just *us*. I mean he doesn't like Maoris." He raised his head cautiously and looked at his mother, but she had picked up her pen again and was doodling on the cover of her pad. She'd felt all along there was something behind this invitation business, but she hadn't expected this, and here she was taken unawares with a mind like a cheap department store. She wondered, with a sudden sense of having failed somewhere, how long it had been going on without her noticing something was wrong, and why hadn't George told her? She'd have to get to the bottom of it now.

"Tell me, Georgie," she said carefully, "have you been having trouble at school over this?" and she glanced up from her doodling. George nodded.

"Yes, I have, a bit. Some of the boys don't like Maoris."

"And this Michael — what's his name?"

"Caine."

"This Michael Caine is one of them?" George nodded again.

"You know that play I told you about, the one where me and Albert were first and second natives?"

"Yes, I remember, it was a good play," Mrs Harrison replied, watching his face. He didn't look uncomfortable any more, now that he'd started talking. "Go on."

"Well, ever since then, Michael and a few of the boys, but mostly Michael, keep on calling us first and second natives …"

"Do you mind being called a native?" put in his mother quickly. George shook his head.

"No, of course not, not in the way you mean," and his mother looked down at her doodling hurriedly. He was so sharp, she'd have to be careful. "They aren't calling us real natives, like the ones you said belong to the land and all that, and they aren't just remembering the play or joking either. They say it — well —" he screwed his face up again and scratched an ear, "well — as though we're dirty or got something the matter with us," he finished lamely.

"A term of abuse," Mrs Harrison murmured to herself. "And what does Albert do? He's much darker than you."

"Oh, he cheeks them back, calls them pink and white pigs and things like that. And he's a much better fighter than I am," he added thoughtfully. Mrs

Harrison's grip on her pen tightened and she jabbed at the doodle. "But I know he doesn't like it even though he says it's only cheek," went on George in the same thoughtful voice, "and when he told his mother — gee, she went nearly raving mad. The trouble with them is," he said, smoothing his comic out with a frown, "I don't think they'd like to be called any kind of natives, not even real ones." Mrs Harrison nodded understandingly.

"Yes. I know what you mean. I've noticed that about Albert. It's a pity." She laid the pen down and propped her elbows on the table. "But listen, George, if this Michael Caine is so nasty, and silly — and he *is* being silly, you know," she said pointedly, "because he doesn't know what he's talking about — why on earth do you want to ask him to your birthday party?" George's face brightened and he propped himself on his elbows too.

"Well, I read in a comic once, Mum, about a chap who had an enemy, and he invited this enemy to stay with him for the holidays, and after that they weren't enemies any more because they'd got to know each other properly." Mrs Harrison watched him with slow misgivings as he went on eagerly. "And I thought if Michael could come to the party and have a good time and see what we're like and all that, he'd stop being such a — so silly. I think it might work, Mum. You know all the kids want to get invited to my parties. They say they're beaut fun and you're so good at making pies and things."

"Well, that's something," smiled his mother feeling ridiculously pleased with herself, "but there's one thing, George, about your plan. Because it worked in the comic doesn't mean it's going to work here. And what if it doesn't, what will you do then?"

"I know," he muttered, his face clouding over again, "I've thought of that. That's why I couldn't make up my mind." They looked at each other for a moment.

"But I'd like to give it a go all the same," he said finally, "and if it doesn't work, I'll never ask him again."

"Okay," nodded his mother, picking up the pen, "Michael Caine it is. Now if you can be in bed by the time I've done this, you can finish reading that story."

The Saturday of the party was fine, which was something, thought Mrs Harrison as she went over in her mind the twelve hours that lay ahead, but the promising morning rapidly developed into a series of last-minute hitches and disappointments. George opened his presents from the family straight after breakfast, and the windjacket with the fur collar from his grandmother, which he knew he was getting and had counted on wearing that afternoon, was too small and had to be wrapped up again for taking back to the shop. The book his grandfather sent him was one he already had, and the pocket microscope from his father proved to be much more difficult to manipulate than it had seemed in the shop. Only his mother's gift, a blue and yellow plastic glider with a marvellous wingspan of eighteen inches, was an unqualified success. Then the telephone began ringing. One boy couldn't come and another wasn't sure. His favourite aunt, who had promised to be at the birthday tea and bring a surprise with her, was sorry she couldn't possibly manage it, but if she came on Sunday instead would he save her a piece of cake? And worst of all, in the middle of lunch his father was called away urgently and had no idea when he would be back, though probably not till late that night. George had grown quieter and quieter as the long morning dragged on and, after his father had gone, had buried himself in a comic as though he had forgotten it was his birthday and there was to be a party and a plan to carry out. His mother left him alone till half past one before she jollied him into clean clothes and his best jersey and gave him some of his father's brylcreem, and then she sent him off with enough money to shout the other boys at the local cinema. "Have a good time," she called after him as he went down the path, "tea will be ready when you all come back." By four o'clock everything was prepared — cheerios in the pot on the stove, little meat pies keeping warm in the oven, bowls of fruit salad on the bench, the table crowded with sandwiches chocolate rice bubbles fancy biscuits chippies lollies bottles of fizz and the big cake with *Happy Birthday George* in silver letters encircled by ten red candles. She checked the number of plates and straws, put some paper serviettes handy in case they wanted to take home what they couldn't eat, and made herself a cup of tea. She felt nervous and on edge. It's ridiculous, she told herself as she changed into the dress George liked best and did her face and hair, after all, who is this wretched Michael Caine? Just a cheeky little boy who needs to be taught a thing or two. And if George's plan doesn't work — so much the worse for Caine. It would be his loss, not theirs. But the nervousness persisted, grew worse if anything, and she was almost glad when she heard voices coming up the path. Once things got under way she'd be all right.

Albert burst through the back door, slammed it behind him and flung himself into a chair.

"First up," he panted, and ran an experienced eye over the table of food.

"Gee I love those chocolate rice bubble things."

"Good," Mrs Harrison smiled, straining the cheerios over the sink, "there are plenty more."

"Hullo," called George from the back porch, and the others bundled into the kitchen and stood staring at the table.

"Mum, you know Dan and Graham, don't you?" and the two boys jostled each other and grinned sheepishly at Mrs Harrison. "Andrew didn't turn up, and this is Michael Caine."

"Ah," said Mrs Harrison, smiling carefully, "I've heard quite a lot about you, Michael, I'm glad you could come to George's party." Michael didn't seem interested in the food like the others and stood staring about the kitchen at the gleaming floor, gaily painted cupboards, stainless steel bench, flowers in the window, but now he glanced sharply up at Mrs Harrison. Big for his age or older than the rest, she thought, still smiling at the straight fair hair and blue eyes, and he's sharp — too sharp and cocky.

"Well, thanks for asking me, Mrs Harrison," he answered, and looked past her at the shining bench. "You know," he said, nodding towards it, "my mother's got a bench just like that. You've got a nice place here, Mrs Harrison."

"Yes, haven't we?" she beamed at him, "Now come along and sit up, the cheerios are getting cold. Michael, will you sit over there next to George …"

"Can I sit next to George too?" Albert asked quickly.

"Of course. You sit on this side, and Graham, you're next to Michael, and Dan next to Albert. Right? Now — two four six eight."

"Bog in, don't wait!" shouted the boys, and grabbed at the food.

"What was the film like?" asked Mrs Harrison, moving round the table and taking the tops off the bottles.

"A real beaut," Albert exclaimed through a mouthful of cheerios. "You see, these settlers wanted to buy some land from the Indians, but the Indians wanted to keep it for themselves, so …"

"… the settlers shot the Indians — pow! pow!" interrupted Michael.

"Shut up, Caine," Albert growled. "Who's telling this story?"

"Anyway, a lot of the settlers got shot too," said George shaking his bottle to make it fizz.

"But the settlers won," Michael persisted, helping himself to the last pie. Albert glared at him.

"Nobody won. They just made a sort of agreement …"

93

"... so the settlers could have the land," finished Michael. "That's what really happened, didn't it, Mrs Harrison?"

"I'm afraid I don't know much about early American history, Michael," she replied, not looking at George and Albert, "but it must have been something like that. Now, who'd like another pie?" and she took a fresh tray out of the oven.

"What about you, Graham? You're being very quiet over there, and you too, Dan." Dan and Graham had been methodically working their way round the table while the others wasted time arguing, but they barely glanced at the assortments already on their plates before reaching up for the tray Mrs Harrison lowered over their heads. Somehow, Michael's bottle of fizz was sent flying and a good half of the drink gurgled over his plate and splashed down the front of him.

"You clumsy clot, I'll get you for that," he threatened, holding a clenched fist over Graham's head. Graham shrank back in his chair, giggling nervously.

"Never mind, Michael," Mrs Harrison said quickly. "I've got an extra bottle you can have. Would you like to come to the bathroom and wipe that off?"

"Yes, I suppose I'd better," he muttered, looking down at his dripping clothes, and followed her out of the room. George and Albert exchanged glances.

"Here," Mrs Harrison handed him a dampened towel, "rub it with this and it mightn't stain." Michael looked at it dubiously. What had his mother said about not using the towels? He shook his head.

"It's all right, thanks, I'll use my handkerchief," and he pulled one out of his pocket, passed it hastily over the wet patches and hurried back to the kitchen. All the pies and cheerios and most of the sandwiches had gone. Albert was monopolising the chocolate rice bubbles and Dan and Graham were busy cleaning up the biscuits. George emptied the last of the chippies on to his plate and called out to his mother.

"Mum, what about the fruit salad? We're still hungry."

"Good heavens," she exclaimed, "I forgot all about it," and she handed the bowls round the table. Michael didn't want any.

"Are you sure? Well, how about a chocolate rice bubble?" She removed the plate from under Albert's nose and held it out.

"No thanks. I don't like the smell of them," he replied, looking hard at Albert. Albert stopped munching and looked back.

"Perhaps you'd like a white bread sandwich instead," Mrs Harrison said crisply, in spite of herself, and turned away to the bench. Michael glanced at her back and dug an elbow in Graham's ribs.

"That's right," he whispered loudly, "eat up like a good boy. Here, let me help you," and he tipped the bowl of fruit salad into Graham's lap.

"I'm sorry, Mrs Harrison," Graham stammered nervously, "but my fruit salad — I didn't …" Mrs Harrison swung round and caught Michael's grin.

"That's all right, Graham," she soothed, "scoop up what you can with your spoon and then go to the bathroom. George, I think it's time you lit the candles." She handed him a box of matches. "Ready? *Happy birthday to you, happy birthday to you …*" The others joined in, Michael roaring like a bull, and George pretended he was shy and hid under the table.

"Come on first and second natives," Michael shouted over the smoking candles, "how about a haka? The one that's got *whaka* something in it," and he grinned knowingly at Dan who choked on a mouthful and started to laugh and thought better of it. Albert was on his feet, leaning across the table and glaring at Michael under straight black brows.

"Shut your face, Caine," he shouted back, "or I'll shut it for you, you pink pig." George looked at his mother.

"Sit down, boys," she said firmly, "while George cuts the cake and makes his wish." George plunged the knife in recklessly. "And Michael, if you want to hear some Maori — *whakarongo mai, fermez la bouche.*" She looked at him steadily.

"Gee — listen to that," breathed Michael, opening his eyes wide. "What's it mean, Mrs Harrison?"

"It means the pig is in the pigsty," she said lightly and laughed. "Now off you all go into the sitting-room and look at the presents while I wrap up a piece of cake for each of you to take home."

When she went through to the front room with the cake, Michael was standing by the windows examining the glider and the others were trying to work the microscope.

"Here you are boys," she said, "and I think it's time to go now."

"Can't we have a game, Mum," George pleaded, "just one. We always do." His mother made a show of looking at her watch. She'd had enough, and it didn't matter what the real time was, it was still time for them to go. And then she remembered the plan.

"Well, I suppose, just one," she gave in reluctantly, "but only for five minutes, so let's have something short and simple. How about Simon Says, and I'll give the winner sixpence. How's that?"

"Yippee."

"Spread yourselves out so you won't hit each other. Dan, you might put an arm through the window if you stand there. That's better. Now, are you all ready? Simon says — do *this*, Simon says — do this — do *this*." Dan went out almost straight away and Graham followed suit soon after. But George and Michael and Albert copied her movements like three well-drilled soldiers moving as one man, and no matter what she did she couldn't trick them into a wrong move.

"I give up," she said at last, "I'll never get you three out."

"Please, Mum," George pleaded once more, "you can't have three winners. Just one more go."

"All right, I'll try to make it harder," sighed his mother. "The last man's out. Ready? Simon says —" and that time George was a split second behind the others. He sat down without a word and concentrated on Albert.

"You two don't want to go on, do you?" Mrs Harrison asked hopefully. They nodded without taking their eyes off her and she looked at their strained faces and tense bodies and wished she hadn't been such a fool to suggest a competitive game, she might have known this would happen. It didn't matter who won, there was bound to be trouble whichever one it was. She looked at her watch and pretended surprise.

"Do you know we've been playing for fifteen minutes instead of five? I declare myself beaten and you two the winners," she smiled, "and I owe you sixpence each." Michael and Albert glanced at each other, but took their money without a word. "Now it really is time to go. Don't forget your cake," and she ushered them out the front door and watched them troop down the steps. George picked up his glider and followed them.

"I'll see them down to the road," he told his mother, "and then I might give her a try-out on the back lawn." She nodded understandingly. After the performance at the tea table, who'd want to share a new glider with that lot.

George stopped before he got to the gate and watched his friends disappear round the other side of the hedge.

"Bye! See you on Monday," he called out, and turned back up the path. He wasn't sorry to see them go. It had been a good party, but next year perhaps he'd just have Albert, and his mother might let him stay the night and they could pack some food and go for a tramp over the hills or something. Suddenly something struck him between the shoulder blades and he wheeled round with a gasp to find Michael on the step behind him.

"Got you," he grinned, "time you had your ears cleaned out, Harrison."

"Oh, I heard you all right," George lied, trying not to show that he'd got a fright, "but I wanted to see what you'd do. What do you want? Forgot something?"

"Nope." He moved up beside George and looked at the glider. "I heard you say you were going to give her a try-out and I thought I'd have a go too." George shook his head and backed slowly up the next step. The sneak — creeping up on him like that.

"I've changed my mind. Too many trees around here. It needs plenty of space like a park …"

"Aw — come on," Michael cut in impatiently, "you're just trying to put me off," and he twitched the glider out of George's grasp, poised it in one hand at shoulder level while he fended George off with the other, and then launched it down the path. George held his breath as he watched it swoop straighten out rise again curve suddenly with a flash of yellow wings like some tropical bird, watched it crash high against a tree and fall to the ground in two pieces. He let out a cry and bounded down the steps to where it lay. Michael followed slowly with a worried frown. He'd only wanted to have a go — hadn't meant to break it. How was he to know it could turn like a boomerang? It had been a good party, almost as good as the chaps at school said it would be, and he was glad he'd come in spite of his mother's warnings. And now this had to happen. Not much chance of being asked again.

"Look what you've done, Caine," George cried, his voice shrill with anger and the desire to weep, "you've wrecked it — wrecked it." Michael peered at the broken pieces George was trying to fit together with trembling fingers, and mumbled something, but George wasn't listening.

"I wish I'd never asked you to my party, I wish I'd asked Peter instead." His voice broke. "Look at it — finished. I've got a good mind to tell my mother who did it, you clumsy clot." Michael coloured angrily and clenched his fists.

"Who wants to come to your lousy parties anyway? Simon Says and all that kid stuff!" He hunched his shoulders and brought his face close to George's. "And you can tell your mother something else too. Tell her I said she's a dirty stinking brown cow of a Maori, and see what she can do about it." George lashed out at him blindly, missed, and stumbled to his knees as Michael dodged back.

"Yaa ..." he jeered, retreating down the steps, "missed — first native missed. What are you on your knees for? Better go and see mammy, and don't forget what I said." And then he was gone. George picked himself up, collected the pieces of glider and made his way slowly up the path, but the steps seemed too high and his knees shook and his chest didn't want to go on breathing. He sniffed once and wiped his nose along his sleeve. What could he tell her, what was he going to say? She was running water and clattering dishes in the sink and didn't hear him come in the door behind her. He put the broken glider on the table and slumped in a chair, waiting, and suddenly she looked round startled, as though he had called out.

"Hello, George, I didn't hear you come in. How long have you been there?" Her eyes narrowed and she came across to the table wiping her hands on her apron. "What's the matter?" and then she saw the glider and frowned. She'd gone to some trouble choosing it, discussing wingspan and flexibility and weight and heaven knows what else, until the shop assistant had left her talking to herself and gone away to serve another customer. And after all that it hadn't lasted him a day.

"How did that happen? I didn't think you'd break it so soon. What a pity." She couldn't keep annoyance out of her voice. George looked at her present.

"It was Caine," he said dully, "he crept up behind me and grabbed it and threw it against a tree." His mother's frown deepened and she made a noise in her throat.

"The clumsy clot. What did he want to do that for?" She looked up when George didn't answer and saw his face. Exhausted, she thought and no wonder. "Well, never mind, I'll see if I can get you another next time I go to town. How's that?" Still no answer. "George, did you hear what I said? I'll get you another ..." He moved restlessly in his chair and looked out the window.

"It's not just the glider, it's the plan — it didn't work." His mother sat down opposite him and pushed the broken toy to one side.

"How do you know? Did he say something?"

"He said it was a lousy party, just kids' stuff, and he didn't want to come to any more." Mrs Harrison sniffed and straightened the crumpled tablecloth.

"That suits me just fine, and I couldn't care less what he thinks about the party. But that doesn't spoil your plan, does it? I mean, it's not what we were talking about when I was doing the invitations." George looked at her miserably. Her hair had got messed up when she was playing Simon Says and most of her make-up had worn off leaving her forehead and nose shiny and slightly greasy and her lips pale inside what was left of her lipstick. Tiredness deepened the lines and hollows of her face and she looked old.

"He called me first native again, and then ..." he turned away to the window once more, "and then he said I was a dirty stinking brown Maori." His mother watched him closely for a minute. He was shaken and she'd have to do something about it, restore his confidence in what he was, even if it meant taking a leaf out of Albert's book.

"George, tell me, what is Michael Caine?"

"A pig," he replied flatly without hesitation, "just a pig."

"That's right, and he doesn't know any more than a pig, and when he calls you or Albert or anyone else names, he's only grunting. Do you see?" and she smiled at him inquiringly. George nodded and forced a lopsided smile back. He was tired, so tired he wished it could be tomorrow — or yesterday. "Now I'd better finish those dishes," his mother said, and stood up, "and will you gather all your presents in the sitting-room and see if you can find places for them in your bedroom?"

"Okeydoke, Mum," he managed to sound cheerful, and did a sort of hop step and jump out of the room and down the passage. His mother watched him go with some surprise. That had been easier than she'd expected, or perhaps he hadn't been as upset as she thought, in which case she'd overdone the pig business. She moved over to the sink and turned on the tap. Oh, well, what did it matter as long as she'd helped him get things sorted out in his mind. George stood in the middle of the sitting-room and stared blindly at the pile of presents on the sofa. And then he scooped them up in his arms all higgledy-piggledy, string and paper too, and did his act down the passage again, and shut his bedroom door carefully with one shoulder, and leaned against it and wept.

Jerusalem, Jerusalem

If my date hadn't been late that Friday night I wouldn't be telling you this, because I wouldn't have met Olive instead and found out what I did. A brisk southerly had been hosing down the city all day, leaving it brighter and darker and taller and wider than it ever really is, and excited in a shivering jittery kind of way, like a dog that has just had a bath it didn't want. It certainly wasn't the night for a leisurely stroll down town or to be loitering in shop doorways, and yet a surprising number of the city's population were doing just that. There were the usual pub leftovers and the picture crowd and the ones who like eating late in Chinese restaurants and the others who would later take up residence in the coffee shops if they hadn't managed to gatecrash a party. And there were exhausted housewives, weighed down with the weekend shopping and drooping on tram stops, while bright young things, all eyeshadow and stiffened petticoats, clung to their Valentinos and hastened towards Romance. Some of the shops had closed already, hustling their customers and assistants outside where husbands waited with pale-faced children and boyfriends shuffled impatiently and dropped half finished cigarettes and stood on them. And as though the natives weren't more than enough, two American ships had berthed that afternoon and the pavements were awash with sailors and girls like gaudy tropical fish. I was afraid of missing my date in that crowd, so worked my way round the traffic lights twice, just in case, hopping from one side of the road to the other whenever the greens gave me the chance, as a child jumps from rock to rock when the waves suck back and wait, and trying to gain a foothold on each corner was worse than landing on a slippery ledge with someone standing in the way. In the end I gave up, and elbowed myself into the doorway of Madame's exclusive gown salon. I wriggled into the black satin cocoon in the window and went to the party and had a fabulous time and came back on the stroke, like Cinderella, to find a little fox terrier man thumping a newspaper tail against his thigh and snapping at my legs, have a drink have a drink come and have a drink. The last corner, which was also the first, proved to be the best. I backed up against a wall of marcasite and New Zealand souvenirs, wondering how much pressure plate glass can take to the square inch, and then I saw Olive. I never know why some faces stand out in a crowd, but they do, and the shifting shapeless mass suddenly becomes a background to one small oval of meaning, and the shock of recognition is so great, you hail a mere acquaintance as though he were a beloved uncle, and then you have to turn away quickly to hide your excitement while you try to remember his name. Olive had such a face, and my heart leapt and flipped over and went through all the gymnastics hearts are supposed to be capable of, when I saw it. Not that she was a close friend of mine or ever had been, even in the old days, but she belonged to the brightest of my childhood, and who can stand on a street corner and not tremble as the past walks out of a crowd?

I don't know how long the Kellys had been at the Bay before I first saw them. A public works camp had come from nowhere and dug itself in on the outskirts of our small community, and it was hard to keep track of all the new faces. The 'permanent residents', as they called themselves, didn't like the invasion one bit. I think they feared deep down it was the beginning of the end, and in a way, I suppose it was. They used to go to the local store in twos and threes and pretend they couldn't think what they wanted and turn to the nearest stranger and say, "I'm not in a hurry, you go first," and then stand back and watch while their victim blushed and stammered and the woman behind the counter who didn't want to lose any old custom on account of the new because you can't depend on PWCs, would go to the fridge at the other end of the room and call out, "did you say half a pound of butter?" One of these sessions was in full swing the afternoon I found Billy and Ken sitting on the ground beside the store door with their backs against the wall. Now that tickled me. We local kids used to get up to all kinds like turning somersaults on the rail at the top of the steps and accidentally kicking people as they came out, and dressing up a dog and taking it for a walk in a borrowed pram, and leaving dead wetas beside the seat in the Ladies. But we never, not ever, sat on the ground outside the store and put our backs to the wall. So I sauntered past them and back again, humming carelessly to myself, and stopped to look at the view, and turned a somersault or two, and I liked them. Liked the way they sat and grinned and nudged each other and whispered in something like Maori, but it wasn't and I even liked the way they soon lost interest and ignored me. And then the woman came out, and it was my turn to lose interest in them. She was tall and dark and thin, and had a thing like a bright cotton curtain wrapped around her somehow and hanging right down to her large bare feet. I looked again, *bare* feet and her toes sort of spread out and flapped a bit as she walked away. I was goggling after her open-mouthed, and wondering if she really walked differently from us or if it was only because of the curtain thing round her legs, when Billy and Ken scrambled up and raced after her, laughing and shoving each other as they went. Inside the store the postmortem had already begun, and everyone was fairly clamouring to get her knife in. *What a get-up have you ever never in my whole life they say he's white can you imagine what next.* And the woman behind the counter who had her shoes specially made (glacé kid, you know) because of her bunions, and always wore corsets for her weak back (you could see where they stuck into her middle when she bent over), fanned the air in front of her as though someone had made a bad smell, and vowed she had never, *never,* had such a — such a *creature* inside her shop before.

When Billy and Ken came to school, and that was some time after the store, they brought two sisters with them. Mary was olive and pink and very shy and had her mother's straight blue black hair. Judy was brown and round and curly and her teeth were appalling. The four of them had enormous black eyes and could use them like gimlets when they wanted to. Our school was one room with a porch for coats and two teachers and a paddock with pine trees at the far end, and whatever we did, we all did it together, because there weren't enough of us to split up into gangs. So when some brought bags of marbles, they'd be shared out, and at playtime the whole school would play, and the little ones who were too young, like Mary and Judy, would yell and jump about and get in the way. Billy and Ken were very good at marbles. They would crouch in the dust like cats and open their eyes wide and let fly, and whenever they scored a hit and they nearly always did, you'd wonder the glass could stand it. But our favourite game was rounders. Every lunchtime, unless it rained and sometimes even then, the man teacher, who was young and liked to keep fit, would come out swinging the round bat and divide us into teams and toss for it and scatter the fielders round the paddock. Then he would tuck his trousers into his socks, like plus-fours, and lead the batting side and tear round the field roaring like a bull, "out of my way out of my way," and we'd fall over ourselves laughing and roll in the grass and laugh and laugh because we loved it and he looked so funny. And on very wet days, after we'd finished our sandwiches, we'd sit round the old stove in the corner and have a community sing, and the woman teacher would warble, "D'ye ken John Peel", and if we didn't, she'd shout the words at us, stamping on the beat till she was red in the face and her fronts flopped up and down. There were a few lunchtimes when both teachers were too busy to keep an eye on us, and we'd sneak down to the out of bounds pine trees and play apes, and Billy and Ken would swing the farthest and hang the longest and make the worst faces, till someone thought they heard the bell, and then it was *slither* and torn clothes and hands and a race across the paddock not to be the last one in. I don't know how those two teachers stood that job, because, in the classroom, even more than in the playground, whatever we did, we *had* to do it together. There wasn't anywhere else to do it. But they stood it, all right, and if the new ones, and there were several besides the Kellys, had hopes that they wouldn't be noticed in the confusion that was us working, they didn't have them for long. Mary and Judy had practically no English and the boys were loath to use what little they had preferring expressive grunts instead, but they were all extremely quick on the uptake, only they didn't let on. If that teacher had realised what was going on behind the grunts and solemn eyes, she might have saved herself many patient painstaking hours, or taught them more than she did. On the other hand, she might have given up the job altogether. I was on the other side of the room and didn't see much of them during classes, but every afternoon I found out what they had absorbed during the day, because as soon as we were clear of the school gate they started to chant it, finding the rhythm in it and stamping it all the way down the hill to the beach. And Ken, who was a wicked mimic, would caper before us, and be that poor teacher.

Although Tom Kelly had a public works job like most of the newcomers to the Bay, the family lived down on the beach instead of up at the camp. It might have been that there weren't enough army huts to go round, or it might have had something to do with what happened at the store. Or perhaps he was just trying to make his wife and children feel at home in their new country, though I shouldn't imagine that the Bay, even the beach part of it, would have much in common with Apia. Anyway, whatever the reason, he had taken a house at the foot of the big hill, and Mrs Kelly had used all she had to make it into a home. The all consisted of several finely plaited mats, a few beautifully polished coconut bowls, a table and chairs, some crockery and cooking utensils, nearly enough beds and bedding to go round, and the old gramophone. After these had been arranged in the living-room facing the sea and the three bedrooms and the dummy kitchen, there was still plenty of room to move about. No matter what time of day I went to that house, and I practically lived there, Mrs Kelly was nearly always out the back preparing food. The kitchen was a dummy one because it didn't have any of the things you'd expect to find in it, like a stove and sink and water and cupboards, so she had made herself a cookhouse with some corrugated iron and a fireplace of stones from the beach, and if we couldn't find her inside when we came in from school, she was bound to be out there in the space between the side of the house and the tin fence, sitting on her haunches and poking and stirring and wiping her eyes with the back of her hand when the fire smoked. She could sit like that, on her haunches with the long skirt wrapped around her thighs, for hours. I don't know what she did for company when we weren't there because she never went out, not even to the store after the first time, and didn't have any visitors because her English wasn't good enough. But she had plenty to keep her busy. There were the mats to shake and water to fetch and clothes to wash and driftwood to be gathered. We used to do what we could to help, like going messages and sweeping the path with a manuka broom, but it wasn't much, and Olive, who was much older than us, had to leave first thing in the morning for the factory in town and didn't get back till late. We hardly saw her except at the weekends, and then if she was in a good mood she would call us to her bedroom and rub coconut oil into our scalps and whack them with a brush till it hurt, and let us play with her nail polish and powder till we got silly and made a mess, and then we were bundled out and the door closed. And sometimes when we were tired of the beach or it was raining and we didn't know what to do with ourselves, Mrs Kelly would line us up in the living-room and show us how to do the siva, gliding and turning and dipping before us like a bird, and her hands were flowers folding and unfolding and folding again. We used to giggle at first and push each other and pretend we were shy, but the bird and the flowers went on beckoning beckoning, and slowly, one by one, we would follow, gliding and turning and dipping and folding, till we weren't us any more, only birds and flowers. Then Mrs Kelly would snap her fingers and stop and smile at us, and the boys would whoop and fall on their backs and kick their legs in the air while we thumped them and thumped them. But of all things we did in that house, the boys liked playing the old gramophone best. They would pull it out from the corner and crank the handle and put on 'Jerusalem, Jerusalem', and while it was playing, they'd sit cross-legged on the floor like stone images and gaze out the window and gaze out the window, with wide darkening eyes. And when it was finished, they'd crank again and put on the 'Hawaiian War Chant' and leap about the room and shake themselves as though they wanted to get rid of their arms and legs. Then they'd go back to 'Jerusalem.' I used to feel uncomfortable about this at first. Hymns meant standing up in church in your hat and gloves, and not knowing the meaning of the words half the time, and watching the choir move their mouths about as though they had toffee sticking to their back teeth. Or they could be your mother trilling in the kitchen like a canary as she prepared breakfast on the mornings she felt good. But they didn't have anything to do with cranky old gramophones and Hawaiian war chants and sitting cross-legged on the floor and listening. Nothing at all. It took me quite a while to get the hang of it.

We played in the house, but we lived on the beach. And we did the kinds of things all children do on beaches, like playing French cricket with a bit of old fruit case for a bat, and writing our names and the date in the damp sand with a stick, and skimming flat stones on the water and counting the hops, and throwing seaweed and old fish heads at one another. But we used to get tired of these, and then we'd really *do* something, like making a Map or a Plan and going on a Hunt. We often went on a Hunt, because if we were lucky, it would end up being a Feast. There were small purple crabs under the rocks nearest the house and big red ones in the deep channels further out and paua at low tide and sea eggs if you knew where to look. The biggest crab we ever caught was a real red whopper, like a small cray, but we didn't eat him. We had been hunting all afternoon and made a good haul and taken it up to the cookhouse, and Mrs Kelly poked our prize catch among the glowing embers and we squatted behind her and smelled the lovely smell and hugged our knees against our chests and grinned at one another. She had raked him out to one side to cool and we were saying who'd have which part, when Tom Kelly looked round the corner of the house. He hardly ever came home till well after our bedtime, but there he was, looking at us without a word, and then he walked over to our Feast and picked him up and took off the back and crammed it all into his mouth at once. And the red legs dangled below his yellow moustache and wiggled up and down as he munched and munched. So we had the sea-eggs instead, and I bolted seven, because of the crab, and was sick all that night. But he never found out about our Plan. The Bay was really three small bays, and we had explored every rock and pool of it except the ones we couldn't reach, and sometimes we would sit in the sand and screw up our eyes against the sea glare and gaze at the part we didn't know and wonder what it was like, out there. And one day we couldn't stand it any longer and that's when we made our canoe. We built it with corrugated iron and the ends of fruit cases and bits of old sacking, and Mary and Judy kept a lookout for grown-ups because they were bound to say I don't think that's a very good idea, and we used to be careful about hiding it under branches and clumps of seaweed, though no grown-up who was really grown-up would have guessed it was any kind of a boat. Early one good calm morning when we had the beach to ourselves we launched her, and she floated away from our proud hands like a log. She could take only one of us at a time, so our Plan was for the first one to sail out the first bay and round into the second, and the second one to sail out the second bay and round into the third, and to come back the same way and do it again, till each one of us had sailed round all the bays. And that's what we did, only we didn't sail, we paddled. The one whose turn it was would get in gingerly and the others steadied her and handed him the fruit case paddles and gave him a bit of a push in the right direction and clambered over the rocks trying to keep level with him, just in case, and shouted look out mind the seaweed, while he paddled like mad to get round before she filled up. So we found out what it was like, out there, and the Great Octopus who lived in the Deep Water beyond the Last Rock jerked and writhed and bulged his eyes with rage as we slopped and wobbled by.

That was summer. Winter brought the bulldozers and the rain and the mud, in that order, and then a repeat of the same. One afternoon when I came home from the Kellys I found the first of the bulldozers had removed a bank that just happened to be in its way, and half our front lawn and path that just happened to be on top of the bank had gone too. A slab of concrete was still hanging on and jutted out from the new cliff edge like a diving board, but the next morning it wasn't hanging on any longer, and slab by slab our path was turned into diving boards that slipped away and lay like tumbled tombstones in the ruined clay below. And the bulldozers moved on. The Ladies went in a morning and the tennis courts that afternoon. The store was picked up and dumped down in the manuka a hundred yards off the road, and the woman behind the counter vowed she had never, *never* been handled so roughly by anyone before. Some of the 'permanent residents' had left already, shutting windows and locking doors and making sure the power was turned off, after it had dawned on them that the new road was going to be put through their privacy and not over the hills behind. The shrewdest of the PWCs, who had no memories to muddle them like us and found it easier to imagine what the new Bay would be like when the road was finished and the bulldozers carted away, said good riddance to the 'permanent residents' ' backs, and left their army huts smartly and moved into the vacant houses. But they made some bad mistakes, for all their shrewdness, and had to pay for them. There was the bloke who went nosing in the gully that was supposed to be an old Maori burial ground, because someone had told him there was so much greenstone down there you couldn't help tripping over it. Well, he tripped over all right and broke his leg and couldn't climb out, and when they found him two days later he was gone in the head and had to be taken away. And there was the drunk who got lost the night of the storm and went down the hill instead of up and passed out on the second zigzag and was dead of exposure by morning. That was the night our canoe disappeared. And up at the camp someone's baby died of diphtheria before they realised what it was. But while the 'permanent residents' who were trying to stick it out worried about compensation, and the PWCs were busy getting themselves into trouble, we kids had the time of our lives, at least in the beginning. The bulldozers were hard at it when we went to school and we used to crowd round the big shovel, watching the polished teeth bite into a bank and jerk and strain till the clay cracked and gave at last, and was caught up by the grab and dropped into the trays of the waiting trucks. And if we went too close the drivers would shout and wave us back and you could tell they were swearing, though no one could make himself heard above the roar and growling of machines. We were late for school more often than not but it didn't matter, we could always say the road was blocked, and the teachers were so afraid one of us would get bulldozed along with everything else, they never said a word. At three o'clock it was a race to be first through the new cutting, and the smoothed clay was all pale blues and greens and golds running into one another and thick and quiet under our feet like A1 linoleum, and you could walk over it and look back and not see a mark anywhere. Then one of the big boys who did geography said they find diamonds in pale blue stuff, and we used to clamber up the terraced banks and dig with sticks till they snapped and claw with fingers instead and lift the lumps above our heads and dash them open on the ground in case the diamonds were hidden inside, and our nails were always pale blue. Sometimes a machine broke down and was left behind by the others, and we would perch all over it like seagulls and the boys narrowed their eyes and moved their hands about and made the noises just right, only not so loud. But the bulldozers moved on, and we were left with the rain and the lorries churning our A1 linoleum into grey porridge, and there weren't any diamonds, and we didn't like the mess that used to be the Bay, any more than the grown-ups did. It was *change* when you got there and *change* when you got back and having to go the long way round, and those of us who had gumboots and slippers were always getting them mixed up in the school porch and going home with two lefts or none at all and not being able to explain why. And some of the mothers made the boys come to school with their heads wrapped in newspaper, like cabbages, because they were sick and tired of buying a new sou'wester every week. By the time the flu came, the grown-ups were so fed up with everything they couldn't crawl into bed fast enough and turn their faces to the wall, and didn't we kids have to get off our tails then. If we weren't fetching and carrying and trying to cook for our own family, we were doing it for someone else's and no one bothered to say *change* or cared if we lost all our clothes. What with the diving boards slipping faster than ever and my mother in bed, the Kellys had been away from school several days before I had a chance to go down to the beach. And when I did go, I almost wished I hadn't, it was so awful. Olive was staying in town and came home only at the weekend because the new road made it harder to get to the factory on time, and Tom Kelly had moved on with the bulldozers but Mrs Kelly and the four children were there and even I could see they were very sick indeed. They had dragged their beds into the corners to try and keep dry, because the roof didn't leak, it simply let the rain in, and the water was up to my ankles in the dummy kitchen. I couldn't get round to the cookhouse because the bank behind the house had slipped and blocked the back door, but even if there had been some food out there it probably wouldn't have been the right kind for flu. I sat on the end of Mrs Kelly's bed and talked about the weather, but I wasn't sure she understood, her eyes were so bright and strange. And the children didn't want to play even being sick-in-bed games, like I Spy. They just shivered and shivered and put their heads under the thin damp blankets. My mother was too sick herself to do anything, but she gave me lemons and honey and aspirins and cooked food to take down every day. And they recovered slowly, like everyone else, but most of the mats were ruined and the cookhouse was a shambles. Before the children were well enough to go back to school I went down with chickenpox and complications, and by the time I could be wrapped in a chair and put out in the pale spring sunshine, the diving boards had slipped away right up to our front door and my mother said it was time to go. So we left the Bay, and the Kellys, and moved north.

"How many years is it?" asked Olive. I smiled down at the two little girls sharing the handle of her shopping basket, because they were very like Mary and Judy.

"I'm not sure," I replied, pretending to count them, "but too many, anyway." We had stumbled over the awkward preliminaries, the crowds pressing about us and the noise of the traffic, making them even more awkward, and now there was nothing left to talk about except the memories we had in common.

"And how is your mother?" The question had been waiting impatiently on the tip of my tongue all the time. Olive looked at me sharply with surprise, and away again.

"She's dead. It's a wonder you didn't hear about it."

"Oh," I said, and it was my turn to look away, "I'm so sorry," as though I had just trodden on her toe. And my date could have whistled in my ear then, and I wouldn't have known.

"Yes, she died soon after we left the Bay. We moved not long after you, and went north too. But she never really recovered from the flu and that house, especially that house." She made a small grimace at me, and I nodded. "They pulled it down as soon as they got rid of us, and about time too. It was condemned, you know, even before we took it, but Dad was prepared to pay the rent they wanted, so they stretched a point." I leaned against my plate glass, hardly hearing what she said. People had a habit of dying, they were doing it all the time, and it didn't do to forget it.

"And the children," I asked, looking down at the two little girls, "how are the children?" She smiled and put her arm round them.

"You're getting mixed up, aren't you? They aren't like this any more. Judy's got a baby, and Mary," she hesitated, and the smile faded, "well, Mary's been in the san for a while, but she'll be out soon." The children had been listening and watching us with bright dark eyes, and the one like Judy suddenly piped up.

"And Uncle Billy knows all about gaol and tells us, and so does Uncle

Ken, but he's only been there once." Olive shook the child by the shoulder and frowned, and she looked up at her mother, bewildered.

"That's right, Mummy, Uncle Ken's ..."

"That's *enough*," snapped Olive, and nearly jerked her off her feet. There was a long pause, and Olive tilted her chin away from me and watched the sailors and the girls on the other side of the street. The traffic lights blinked and blurred, blinked and blurred.

"What could I do?" she suddenly burst out, facing me furiously though I hadn't said a word, "what would you expect me to do? Dad went back on the public works, and I had my life to live too, didn't I? And a good job at the factory at last."

"Of course," I managed to put in, but she hadn't finished.

"And I used to go out and see them at the orphanage every week, and when they left there I thought they were old enough to look after themselves. And I married a Yank," she fumbled among the parcels in her basket and looked across the street again, "I married a Yank, and he didn't come back." She lifted her shoulders with a deep breath and let it out quickly. "And by that time it was too late. So there's just the three of us," and she looked down at her children. They had been watching us uncertainly since something had gone wrong with the conversation, but now they brightened up again and smiled at their mother hopefully, and Olive smiled at me in spite of herself, and I smiled at the three of them. And one or two people glanced at us curiously as they pushed past, we all looked so happy.

"Well, bedtime at the zoo," said Olive briskly, and the two little girls shook her arm and jigged up and down, crying no, no.

"Yes, I'd better be off too," I said, forgetting all about my date. "It's not the night for hanging around, is it?" And Olive smiled again as she turned away from me for the last time, and half waved before she crossed with the green. And the little girls went hopping and skipping on either side of her, like children on a beach.

Other books by J.C. Sturm

How Things Are (poems, with Adrienne Jansen, Harry Ricketts &
    Meg Campbell; Whitireia Publishing & Daphne Brasell, 1996)
Dedications (poems; Steele Roberts, 1996)
Postscripts (poems; Steele Roberts, 2000)
The Glass House (stories and poems, Steele Roberts, forthcoming)